The Jazz Kid

THE
JAZZ KID

JAMES LINCOLN COLLIER

Henry Holt and Company
New York

Henry Holt and Company, Inc.
Publishers since 1866
115 West 18th Street
New York, New York 10011

Henry Holt is a registered
trademark of Henry Holt and Company, Inc.

Published in Canada by Fitzhenry & Whiteside Ltd.,
195 Allstate Parkway, Markham, Ontario L3R 4T8.

Library of Congress Cataloging-in-Publication Data
Collier, James Lincoln.
The jazz kid / by James Lincoln Collier.
Summary: Playing the cornet is the first thing that twelve-year-
old Paulie Horvath has taken seriously, but his obsession with
becoming a jazz musician leads him into conflict with his parents
and into the tough underworld of Chicago in the 1920s.
[1. Jazz—Fiction.   2. Musicians—Fiction.   3. Chicago (Ill.)—Fiction.
4. Parent and child—Fiction.]   I. Title.
PZ7.C678Jaz   1994   [Fic]—dc20   93-33932

ISBN 0-8050-2821-8

First Edition—1994

Printed in the United States of America
on acid-free paper.∞

1 3 5 7 9 10 8 6 4 2

For Tristan

AUTHOR'S NOTE

Readers should be warned that I have used in this book a few racial and ethnic nicknames, such as "nigger" and "Chink." Today these terms are considered insulting and are generally avoided. But at the time this story took place, they were standard usage in common speech. I have included them for the sake of historical accuracy and because one of the themes of the book is the racial attitudes of the time, but that does not indicate that I encourage their use.

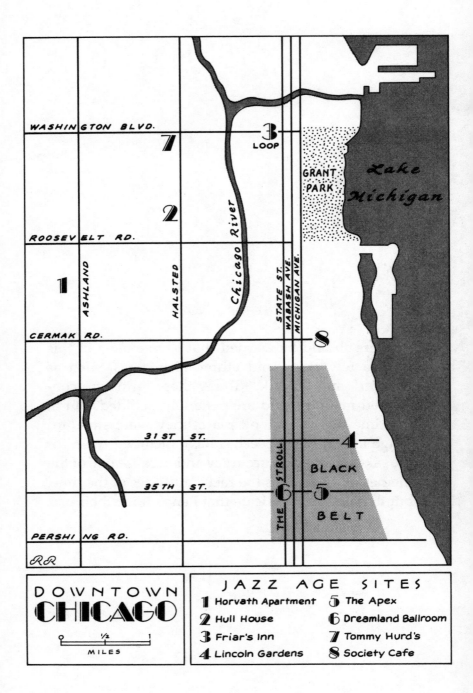

The Jazz Kid

1

THE WAY IT started was, when I was twelve and going into the seventh grade. A couple of days before the Fourth of July, my big brother, John, found out there would be a parade over on Halsted Street. He told Ma he'd take me over if she gave us each a dime for ice cream. Ma said John shouldn't be so greedy for money, he should take me over for nothing, but in the end she gave us each a nickel and we went.

Well, it was a peach all right, that parade. There was a mess of soldiers in brown uniforms marching with their guns held just so and their legs scissoring along together. There were a couple of touring cars filled with old fellas in suits who were left over from some war I was supposed to know about but didn't;

and a whole slew of bands coming along one after another, so that the music from one hadn't died out before the next one took up. For a little while you could hear them both at once, playing different songs at different speeds. John said, "They ought to space the bands out more so you couldn't hear two at once."

But I liked hearing two bands at once. It gave me a thrill up my back for some reason. I don't know why it did, it just did. "What's wrong with hearing two bands at once, John?"

"You can't hear the songs right if they both come together." John was three years older than me and got A's in everything at school.

"I don't care," I said. "I like it that way."

"You would, Paulie," John said. "That's why you always flunk at school."

I still didn't care. I liked hearing them that way, so I stood there as each band passed listening hard for the next one, and sure enough, in about a minute I'd begin to pick up the music of the next band, playing a different song. For a little while there I'd be able to hear both bands at once. I'd close my eyes and listen, just to get that thrill. Then the first band would die out and I'd open my eyes again.

I had them open down toward the end of the parade, when along came a band of kids around my age—maybe a little older. They were wearing the snazziest uniforms I ever did see—on a kid at least— red jackets with gold buttons, blue trousers with gold stripes down the legs, caps with gold initials stitched into them. All of them tootling away on shiny trombones and cornets, banging on golden cymbals and big fat drums. They looked as famous as could be.

Oh, how I wanted to be in that band. Oh, how I wanted to be right down there in the middle of all that confusion of red and gold, the shininess of things, the banging and booming and tootling, the scissoring legs, and the sound of two different songs going on at the same time.

Finally it was over. I looked at John. "John, do you think Ma and Pa would let me get into a band?"

"Pa wouldn't. Ma might. She might figure it would teach you to discipline yourself."

"Maybe it would." I wasn't sure I wanted to learn to discipline myself.

"You'd have to practice your instrument."

"I could make myself practice." I wasn't sure about that, either. But it might be worth it.

John laughed. "Paulie, Ma and Pa have been trying to teach you to discipline yourself all your life. Pa says it's like trying to teach a frog to play the banjo."

I gave him a look. "You'll see, John." But I couldn't really tell John the truth about it, because he'd give me a funny look. Pa had got his mind made up that me and John would come into the plumbing business with him as soon as we finished our schooling, get married, and have nice homes the way he did. John was all for it. "Pa's done the hard part," he always said. "We'll be walking into a good thing." That was right. Pa had come up hard and had to go to work at twelve. Back when John was little Pa worked fourteen, fifteen hours a day to build the business up. They used to live in an apartment with a toilet down the hall. Now we had a nice apartment with an inside bathroom, not down the hall, or out in the backyard, like the Flynns; and a carpet on the living-room floor and lampshades with fringes on them. John liked the idea of all that.

But it was too planned out for me. I wasn't the type of person who liked things planned out. Pa and John were. Pa was always making lists of things he had to do. He was always on us to make lists, too, and John would, at least sometimes. But I didn't—I just didn't like the idea of making lists. Oh, I knew I should. But how could you get yourself to like doing something when you didn't like doing it?

But I liked the idea of being in that band all right, all red and gold, whamming and banging, and two songs going at the same time. So that night at supper I brought it up. Like John figured, Pa was dead set against it. He said, "You never took anything serious in your life. You do lousy at school, you leave your clothes all over the floor, you never remember to take the garbage down. I'm not having you waste your time over music until you get serious about the important things. Look at John—why can't you be more like him?"

I wished Pa wouldn't say that all the time. Pa was

fair, and only spanked me a few times when I was little and richly deserved it, the way Ma put it. And he only docked my allowance when I richly deserved it, too, which was often enough, for I was already into January and it was only July. But he had only one way of looking at things, and it was John's way, not mine.

The funny thing is, if Pa had been all for my taking up music, I probably would have lost interest in it. But the more he argued against it, the more determined I got. When you got down to it, I could have already been studying music. Back when I was in the third grade Ma could already see I wasn't going to be the student type, like John. To cheer herself up about me, she decided maybe I was more the artistic type. Pa said if she meant by that I was bone lazy, she was probably right. "What that boy needs is to have his fanny tanned," he said. "Why can't he follow John's example?"

"Well, he isn't like John," Ma said. "Paulie's got his own view of things. There's nothing wrong with being artistic. Look at Norman Rockwell. Millions of people love his magazine covers and I betcha he makes a ton of money."

Pa grumbled about it, but Ma had got her mind made up that I should take piano lessons. Pa said, "Paulie don't need to take up the piano until he starts doing good in school."

"Paulie *doesn't*," Ma said. Pa was smart enough, but he was brought up hard. Anyway, Ma had her way, and every Wednesday afternoon I went to Miss Quintana's and clanged away at the piano. I kind of liked some of that, too—though not the exercises. I couldn't work up much interest in playing scales over and over. But it was a lot of fun to just sort of fool around on the keyboard, trying out different things to see what they sounded like. It wasn't up to throwing stones at cats with Rory Flynn, or stealing chips of ice off the ice wagon, but it was interesting enough. And it might have took, but we didn't have a piano at home. Pa said he wasn't going to shell out five dollars a week for a piano just so Paulie would have a place to park his used chewing gum. What I got instead was a piece of cardboard with a life-size piano keyboard printed on it. Every night I had to unfold it across the kitchen table and practice scales on it. It was the emptiest thing I ever did—even Ma could see that—but Pa said it suited him just fine, he'd always been partial to music you couldn't hear. If we'd had a real piano I could have fooled around on, I'd have stuck with it—practiced the scales enough to keep Miss Quintana content and fooled around the rest of the time. But we didn't. So I lost interest and finally Ma saw it wasn't any good and let me quit. But those lessons with Miss Quintana paid off in the end, for when I finally got interested in music I had a head start.

So I knew that Ma thought I was the artistic type,

and I might be able to talk her into letting me join a band. If I convinced her, she'd get around Pa somehow.

Ma had a soft spot for me. I think she figured out a long time ago that I was on a different track from other people, and she allowed for it. "You're not a bad boy, Paulie," she'd say. "Just got a mind of your own. But you've got to understand how it looks to other people."

But talking her into it wasn't going to be easy, for I hadn't stuck to the piano lessons and she wouldn't believe I'd stick to the band, either. So I said, "Ma, taking up an instrument would probably teach me to discipline myself, the way Pa always says."

"Ho, ho, ho," she said.

"You sound like Santa Claus," I said.

"Well you better keep it in mind I'm not."

"Honest, Ma, it would teach me self-discipline. I'd have to practice and all." I still felt uneasy about that. There wasn't any way I could be in a band if I didn't practice. Would I be able to make myself do it? Or would I get discouraged by something like the cardboard keyboard?

"Fat chance you'd practice. You didn't before when we were paying twenty-five cents a week for piano lessons."

So I said, "Honest, Ma, I would. How could I practice on a cardboard piano?"

She gave me her squinty look. "There's something fishy going on here, Paulie. You've got something in mind."

"No I haven't, Ma. I haven't got anything in mind. I just want to get into a band." I couldn't tell her it was those flashing colors and that shiny confusion that got me. She'd never understand that.

"I don't trust it," she said. "I never saw the time before when you set out to make work for yourself."

"Please, Ma."

"Oh, all right, Paulie. I'll talk to your pa about it." I could tell she knew she shouldn't have given in, but she had that soft spot for me. She waggled her finger at me. "I'm not promising anything. I'll see. You better start getting good marks in school."

To tell the truth, sometimes I wished I did better at school. It would be more comfortable to be a good kid like John and do things right. But I couldn't make myself. Sitting in school, I'd order myself to memorize all the raw materials of someplace nobody ever heard of, like Costa Rica; and the next thing I knew I'd have shaded in with my pencil the O and A's in Costa Rica, and Miss Hassler would be screaming at me for defacing school property.

Or I'd tell myself to carry the garbage down carefully; and then I'd start studying the way my shadow got bigger and smaller as I passed under the hall light and suddenly there'd be orange peels, egg shells, and coffee grounds all over the hall.

Or hang up my clothes—there's a good example.

The truth was, I didn't like it when my pants and shirts were hung up in a neat row in the closet; I liked it a whole lot better when they were scattered around the room—one shoe under the bed, sock on the floor by the bureau, shirt crumpled up on the table where we did our homework. How could a kid like that ever do good in school, even if it would be more comfortable?

2 I HELD MY breath. There was no telling if Ma would be able to get around Pa or not. I spent a whole afternoon—well, half an afternoon—hanging up my clothes and cleaning up my room, I took the garbage down without spilling it, I even got seventy-eight on my spelling test. I thought about changing it up to eighty-eight, which I could have done easy, but there was a limit on how bad a kid I was willing to be.

In the end it was Rory Flynn who got me into the band. I wasn't supposed to know that, but I did, for one night when they thought I was asleep I heard them talking about it in the kitchen.

Pa said, "If Paulie hasn't got nothing better to do in the afternoons he could sharpen some chisels for me. Or do some schoolwork for a change."

Ma said something, but I couldn't hear it exactly. So I got out of bed, cracked open our door, and crouched there, listening. Oh, I knew it was wrong to spy; but it was me they were talking about, wasn't it?

Pa said, "Or clean up his room. You can't hardly walk in there without stepping on something. He has more clothes laying on his floor than I had the whole time I was growing up."

"I told him to pick up his clothes until I was blue in the face," Ma said. "It's like talking to a wall."

"You should talk to his fanny for him. He might see the point."

"You're off the subject, Frank," Ma said. "When was the last time Paulie came around begging for a chance to accomplish something?"

He didn't say anything for a minute. Then he said, "You got something there."

"For another thing, it'd keep him from spending so much time with Rory Flynn."

"Flynn? Peggy Flynn's kid?"

"The same," Ma said.

"Jesus," Pa said.

It surprised me that Ma knew about me and Rory being pals. I never talked about Rory at home, for Mrs. Flynn drank beer and there wasn't any Mr. Flynn. Somebody must have told Ma about me and Rory. Anyway, that was why Pa decided I could join a band—so I wouldn't spend so much time with Rory.

In a way, I kind of envied Rory. He didn't come from a decent home—no carpet on the floor, didn't sit down to a regular supper every night, but got a quarter from his ma and went down to the delicatessen for stuff. But his ma wasn't always on him about his homework, picking up his clothes and stuff, and he didn't have any pa planning his life for him. You could see why Ma and Pa didn't appreciate me hanging around with Rory.

Of course Ma didn't tell me the idea of joining the band was to keep me away from Rory. She said, "Your pa's dead set against it, Paulie. I told him I'd make you promise to do better in school and if you didn't, that was the end of the band." She bent down so she could stare me straight in the eye—no squinty look this time. "Do you understand that, Paulie? If you don't do better in school, no more band."

Well, I didn't know if I'd be able to do better in school or not, but I figured I'd worry about that later. The important thing was I was going to be in a band, marching along clanging and banging and being famous. It seemed like just the greatest thing. I was excited as could be.

A couple of days later Ma took me over to Hull House, which was near our neighborhood at Polk and South Halsted. Hull House was a real fancy place where they put on all kinds of things for kids—and grown-ups, too. The idea was to help the greenhorns get settled in America. They had English classes, cooking classes, sewing classes. They put on plays, they had sports, they had poetry and painting classes. And of course they had a boys' band. When you got down to it, Ma was right: a lot of it had to do with keeping kids out of mischief.

Hull House was made up of three or four buildings. The one for music was called Bowen Hall. We went down to the band room, where they were having a rehearsal—a whole slew of kids sitting on long benches with their music stands in front of them, tootling. And right away I was disappointed, for the kids weren't wearing uniforms, just their plain school clothes—knee pants and such. Most likely they were saving them up for parades. Still, it was a disappointment.

On top of it, the band director was mighty bossy. He had a mustache, his coat off, his sleeves rolled back, waving his stick around. The kids would tootle away for a minute and then the director would whack at his music stand with his stick and the whole thing would grind to a stop. "You're all hopeless," he'd shout. "Doesn't anyone here know what *pianissimo* means? I've heard cannons softer than that." He'd raise the stick up. "Take it from letter C," and off they'd go again, banging and crashing like a herd of elephants on a rampage. I never heard such a racket.

This guy looked like he was tougher than Pa. How long would I be able to stand being bossed around by him before I started ducking out of practice? But it was too late for second thoughts—not after I begged Ma so hard to take up music.

After a while the director got tired of slashing at the air and telling the kids they were hopeless, and took a break. Ma brought me up to him. It turned out his name was James Sylvester. He looked me up and down. "What's the boy's name?"

"Paulie Horvath," Ma said. "He's desperate to play in a band."

Mr. Sylvester nodded. "They all are. The uniforms always get them."

"It isn't just the uniforms," I said. "I used to take piano."

He nodded. Suddenly he grabbed hold of my chin. "Show your teeth."

I opened my mouth. "Aanngg," I said.

"Just your teeth, not your tonsils. I saw all the tonsils I ever wanted to see conducting the girls' chorus."

I snapped my teeth together and spread my lips, feeling like a horse trying to catch hold of an apple. "Good," he said. "I think we can make a cornetist out of you." He let go of my jaw, and jabbed his finger towards my eyes. "But you have to practice." He gave me a serious look over the finger. "No point in even coming back if you aren't going to practice."

"You hear that, Paulie?" Ma said.

Well, I'd let myself in for it this time, all right. I had nobody to blame but myself. For now I *would* have to practice—there was no way around it. If I hadn't begged so hard I could have gone along with it for a few weeks and then quit. But after Ma'd taken all that trouble—talked Pa around and got me to promise to do better in school, and carried me over to Hull House and everything, I would have to stick it out for a while. I'd outsmarted myself, I could see that. But maybe some good would come out of it. Maybe I could make Ma proud of me for once. That would be nice for a change.

So that's how it started. And for a couple of weeks it was pure misery. Before, when I had heard those kids tootling away in that parade I didn't have any idea how hard it was just to get a sound out of that cornet, much less a note anyone would want to listen to. But after about a week of puffing and blowing, I got so I could get some notes out—pretty wobbly they were, more like a sick cow mooing than music, but notes even so. That encouraged me a little; and I was more encouraged after my third lesson, when I got to where I was playing some little tunes out of the songbook. "Maryland, My Maryland," "Home, Sweet Home," stuff like that. Well, I tell you, Ma was pleased as punch. Once, when I was whacking my way through my tunes she came and stood at the door of our room, listening. And I'll be darned if after a minute she didn't reach up and brush at her eye, like she had something in it. Of course Ma wasn't much more of an expert on music than Pa was, aside from singing in the church choir when she was a kid. Still, when she rubbed her eye that time, it made me swell up so much I could hardly play.

That night at supper she told Pa, "Paulie's doing real well on his cornet, Frank. You should hear him."

"Humph," Pa said. "Let's hope he's doing real good at school, too." But after supper he came into our room and made me play "Maryland, My Maryland" for him. All he said was, "Humph," but I could tell he was kind of surprised. It was those piano lessons, as little practicing as I did for them. They made all the difference, for the hardest part of reading music is getting the time right—quarter rests and dotted eighths and stuff—and I already knew how to do that. For a beginner I was ahead of myself. Even Mr. Sylvester said so. "I'm not saying what you're playing could be considered music, Horvath, but I've heard worse. Keep at it and pretty soon I'll put you in the band and give you the uniform that inspired you with your deep love of music."

It made me kind of proud of myself. I wouldn't say it was the first time I ever did anything right. I was good at baseball—at recess I always got picked second or third after Rory, who had got left back and was a year older than the rest. I was good at sailing paper airplanes—me and Rory would shoot them off his back porch, which was tricky because of the clotheslines. But it wasn't often that I was good at things the grown-ups admired. It was nice having Ma proud of me for a change.

But it wasn't pleasing Ma that kept me plugging away at those rotten exercises. It was remembering that gold and red, that sound and confusion and two bands playing at once. Somehow, that stuff was mine, where the plumbing business and fringed lampshades belonged to Pa and Ma and John. That's why I could tolerate those rotten exercises— they didn't have anything to do with the rest of the family.

Still, practicing wasn't any peck of fun. There was always something new to struggle with—a new key signature, triplets, six-eight time. Each time I started on something new I'd have to fight with myself to get through it. But then, when I had as much of the exercises as I could take, I let myself play some of the tunes I already knew. That was fun, just slinging the notes out there and listening to what they were saying; and if I hit off something real smooth it would kind of excite me that it was *me* who was doing it.

So even though it was a struggle a lot of the time, I'd shove and haul myself through it, for I could see that I was getting somewhere. And I decided to stick it out at least until I got into the band and had my uniform, and played in a parade at last.

So I did. Along about October, Mr. Sylvester told me I wasn't what anybody would call a cornet player, but neither were half the kids in the band, and I might as well join in—I wasn't likely to do enough damage to be noticed. They said the band was likely to parade on Thanksgiving and it always gave a Christmas concert. I figured I might as well stick it out to Christmas. That'd make six months, which was longer than I ever stuck to anything in my life. After that I'd see. Then something happened, and my whole life was changed.

3 WHAT HAPPENED WAS, just before Thanksgiving we had a real cold spell—it can get mighty cold anytime in Chicago. A lot of people weren't prepared for it, and their pipes froze. Well, of course, that was good business for Pa, but it meant he was on the run morning, noon, and night, for everything was an emergency. He even took John out of school for a couple of days; John was fifteen, and Pa trusted him to handle simple jobs by himself. So I had to go with Pa as a plumber's helper.

The night before Thanksgiving around eight o'clock we got an emergency call from a place called the Society Cafe, on De Koven Street. All the pipes in the cellar had frozen, and a couple of them had busted. They had to shut off the water and close the place down, which didn't make the guy who owned the club too happy. John was already on a job, so Pa took me. We lugged the toolboxes over on the streetcar—you had to take a lot of stuff, for you never knew what you might come up against.

The place was a real dump, a one-story wood building with a tin roof, running back from the street. Paint was peeling off the clapboards, and there were green curtains over the windows so nobody could see what was going on inside. Pa climbed up the low stoop and knocked on the door. The guy who opened the door was big—not so much fat as heavyset, black hair slicked back, wearing a camel's hair overcoat. He scowled at Pa. "What took you so long?"

"We came as quick as we could."

"Let's go," he said. He took us around back where there was a cellar door and let us in. It was a mess down there—cold dirt floor, wet brick walls, empty beer kegs giving off an old beer stink, a few busted chairs chucked in a corner, the coal furnace, and just one bare light bulb dangling down from the floor joists above. It was so cold we could see our breath. "Let's get this over with," Pa said.

We set to work—well, Pa set to work and I did the best I could to stay out of his way, except to hand him tools when he asked for them, or hold the bull's-eye lantern where he wanted it. We were going along like this, with Pa cursing to himself a good deal and calling out, "Damn it, Paulie, can't you hold that light so it don't shine in my eyes," when I heard people walking around upstairs.

"Somebody came in up there," I said.

"Never mind them. Where's that one-inch elbow I had a minute ago?"

The footsteps came right over my head. Then I heard a sound I never forgot: a stream of cornet notes suddenly spilling down, like a cascade of little silver balls. The sound froze me dead in my tracks, my mouth open, the elbow clutched in my hand.

"Damn it, Paulie, where's that elbow?"

I came to and gave him the elbow. Then the stream of silver balls came again, this time splashing upwards a little after they hit bottom. My head froze up again. Oh, I knew what it was—a cornet player warming up. But it was the way he hit those notes, just exactly so, that caused my head to stop working. They came out so delicate, light, precise, with just a sprinkling of vibrato dusted on the end of each note.

"Damn it, Paulie, how many times do I have to tell you, move that light around here."

I jumped, suddenly back in that cold, damp cellar again. "I couldn't hear you over that cornet."

"Forget about that cornet. It's just that nigger music. Let's get this job done and get out of here."

What did he mean by nigger music? How could anything that pretty be nigger music? Now from overhead there came the sound of somebody noodling on a piano, running a few scales up and down the keyboard. It was a pretty bad piano—even down there I could tell it was way out of tune. The cornet player peeled off another string of silver balls, and after that there was silence.

"Give me that twine, Paulie."

I handed it to him. Overhead there came the quick tapping of four beats on the floor, and then they were going, just piano and cornet, some kind of music I never heard before, a music that danced along like sunshine flickering on the ripples in a lake. A chill went up my spine and curled across the top of my head.

"Damn it, Paulie. I told you to forget about that nigger music."

"I'm sorry, Pa, I couldn't hear with that music playing."

"Next time I'm going to music your fanny."

I had to get up there and see who was making that music. I just had to. Even if I plain ran on out of there, I had to do it. "Pa, how soon will the toilet be on? I got to take a leak."

"Not till I run this new piece of pipe up. Go take a leak out back."

"It's too cold. I can wait."

"Suit yourself," he said. "Where's that can of grease?"

Oh, I tell you, trying to concentrate on that plumbing job was about the hardest thing I ever did. That music kept pouring down from up there, one tune after the next, slow, fast, in-between. It was funny: sometimes I thought I recognized a tune, and a moment later I wouldn't be sure. The cornet player would hint at things, and then he'd go running off in a different direction. That year "China Boy" was real popular, and in different spots it sounded like they were playing it. But every time I convinced myself, "China Boy" would disappear. Another time I got the idea they were playing "Chicago, That Toddlin' Town," which naturally everybody was singing along the streets then. But I never was really sure.

It didn't really matter what the tune was. What counted was the way that music felt to me, the sparkle that was in it, the funny way it scurried along, going here and there, disappearing behind something and then popping out again. I couldn't believe music could make you feel that way.

Hard as it was, I managed to listen to the music with one ear and Pa with the other, and finally we got the job done—well, Pa got it done. Then he said to me, "If you want to take a leak there's a toilet upstairs. I'll turn the water on, you crack the faucets in the sink and see if everything's okay. While you do that I'll start packing up so we can get out of here."

I didn't have to be told twice, but shot for the rickety old wooden stairs. At the top was a trapdoor. I heaved it up and climbed out. I was behind a bar, which ran along one side of a big room. The place wasn't much fancier than the cellar—an old wooden floor gray from years of mopping, a couple of big ceiling fans for summertime, the green curtains over the windows, a bunch of wooden tables with dirty red-checked tablecloths on them. Across the room from the bar stood an old ruin of an upright piano that reminded me of a horse ready for the boneyard. The only people in the room were the cornet player, who was leaning up against the piano, one leg crossed over the other, while he played; and the piano player, who was colored.

But the cornet player was about nineteen or twenty and had straw-colored hair; so it wasn't nigger music after all. When he saw me pop up from behind the bar he stopped in midstream and took the cornet away from his mouth. "Where'd you come from, kid?" he said.

"We're working on the pipes. They were all froze up."

The piano player swiveled around on the stool, and sat there looking at me. He had a cigar about the size of a baseball bat clenched in his teeth, a derby hat tipped back on his head, and he was wearing a dark blue suit with the coat open so you could see his fancy plaid vest and gold watch chain. He raised his eyebrows at me. "You always spring from midair like that?" He took the cigar out of his mouth so he could chuckle. "Mighty fine trick. Mighty fine."

"I came up from the cellar to check the faucets." I wasn't sure I ought to ask questions, but I figured I was likely to. "Where'd you learn to play that kind of music?"

"What? The jazz?" the piano player said.

"Is that what jazz is?" I'd heard of jazz, but didn't know what it was.

"You never heard any jazz?" the piano player said. "Where you been, hiding in a closet?"

I didn't want to seem like too much of a dope. "I think I heard it, but I wasn't sure."

The piano player tapped the ash off his cigar. "Mighty hard to miss around Chicago," he said. "We had it here eight, ten years, I reckon. They ain't got nothin' like it in New York. Nothin' nowhere near like it."

I knew that if I didn't check out those faucets pretty quick Pa'd swarm all over me. "Were you just rehearsing?"

"Just jamming a little," the cornetist replied. "Herbie said since the place was closed anyway, we could come over and jam." He pointed his thumb at the piano player. "Me and him, we don't get to play together all that much."

I didn't know what he meant by jamming, but I didn't want to look like a dope by asking. "How could you learn to play like that?"

The piano player chuckled. "Can't learn it." He put the cigar back in his mouth and shook his head. "That's a plain fact. You got to get a feelin' for it."

From down below there came a shout. "Paulie, what the hell are you doing up there?"

I leaned over the trapdoor. "I couldn't find the toilet."

"What the hell? It's that door right at the end of the bar."

It surprised me that he knew where it was: he hadn't come up out of that cellar the whole time we were here. "Do you play here all the time?"

The cornetist shook his head. "Sometimes I'm here. Nothing regular."

The piano player chuckled. "Jazz musicians don't play *nowhere* all the time."

The cornetist pointed at the piano player again with his thumb. "He got a nice gig over at the Arcadia Ballroom. I'm here for now. No telling how long it'll last."

"Maybe I could come over and hear you."

The cornet player shrugged. "I doubt if they're going to want any kids in knee pants running around here. This is a pretty rough joint."

"Paulie!"

"What time do you start?"

"It's an after-hours joint. We don't start till midnight. Sometimes don't get out of here till the sun's up."

My heart sank. If only they started around eight or something, I might figure a way to hear them. But there wasn't a chance Ma would let me go anywhere at midnight. "Do you ever play during the day?"

"Yeah, sure. There's tea dances sometimes. You never know when one'll come up."

"Come on, Tommy. We done palavered long

enough." He rolled a series of chords up the keyboard.

"Paulie, get your tail down here." I ran out of there to check the faucets, before Pa ate me alive. But it didn't matter, for finally I'd come across something maybe I could discipline myself about. And I knew for sure that for me the plumbing business was a dead duck.

4

AFTER THAT I couldn't think of anything but the music those guys were playing. It kept going around and around in my brain. I could actually hear it. Of course I couldn't remember exactly everything they played, but I could hear the sound of it, the feeling that was in it, in my head.

But it wasn't good enough just to hear it in my brains. I wanted to hear it for real again. I never wanted anything so bad in my life—never wanted a fielder's mitt or a bike or anything so bad as I wanted to hear that music again.

Naturally, I couldn't rest until I tried to play it myself. As soon as we got home that night I unpacked my cornet and tried to play jazz. I just couldn't do it. I didn't know where to begin. I sat there for a minute, holding my cornet in my lap, and thought about it. I remembered how there always seemed to be a song flickering around in what they were playing—a song that would pop out here and there and then disappear again. I figured the thing to do was to start with a song. I picked out "Maryland, My Maryland," which I knew by heart. Nothing happened. I couldn't figure out how to put the jazz into it, and it came out plain old "Maryland, My Maryland," no different than it ever was.

It was clear that I'd have to study that jazz somehow. But how? Who would teach me? Were there any phonograph records of it? We didn't have a phonograph. They were expensive, and considering that Pa was partial to music you couldn't hear, it wasn't likely that we'd get one in the near future. But there was a phonograph at Hull House, which they used for dancing classes, and Rory Flynn's ma had one. Rory said that when she got to drinking beer she'd put on her favorite songs, like "Danny Boy" and "That Old Irish Mother of Mine," and cry, which cheered her up. So if I could get hold of a record with that kind of music on it, I had places where I could hear it.

Did Mr. Sylvester know anything about it? He might, I figured. I went to the next band practice early and asked him. "Did you ever hear any jazz?"

"Jazz? Sure."

"I wondered if I could learn to play it."

He frowned. "What do you want to mess with that stuff for? It's just nigger music. You'll ruin your lip."

"How'd it ruin your lip?"

"It just does. I know a cornet player, fine player, who took up playing jazz and within six weeks he split his lip right on the bandstand, blood all over his dress shirt. You don't want to mess with that stuff."

I wasn't sure I believed it. "I heard some guy playing a couple of days ago. His lip seemed okay."

"He won't get away with it forever," Mr. Sylvester said. "I'm telling you, Horvath, you'll ruin yourself."

It was clear enough that I couldn't learn jazz from Mr. Sylvester. I had a feeling he didn't know much about it anyway. There had to be somebody around who could teach it to me, but who? The only ones I knew were those guys at the Society Cafe. Could I get that cornet player to give me lessons? I knew there was no point in asking Pa. He'd say it was nigger music, and I shouldn't have anything to do with it. Same with Ma. She wouldn't call it nigger music, because she wouldn't use words like that. She always called them colored people. But she wouldn't like the idea of me having a lot to do with them, whatever you called them. Nor would it do any good to say it wasn't just nigger music, for white people played it, too. They'd say a white man ought to be ashamed for lowering himself that way.

But I couldn't see it their way. How could anything that made me feel that good lower me? I figured there had to be a whole lot of people who agreed with me about jazz. Didn't that piano player say if I hadn't heard of jazz I must have been hiding in a closet? Didn't he say it was mighty hard to miss around Chicago? Ma and Pa were wrong about it, that's all there was to it.

The problem was, I'd finally found something I could take serious, and naturally it was something Ma and Pa wouldn't like. I should have known it would be that way. What I liked about jazz was that, even though it had planning to it, it was a different kind of planning. John and Pa wouldn't have seen the planning, but I did. And I could see that the time was going to come when I'd have to tell Pa I wasn't going into the plumbing business, I was going to be a musician. But I didn't have to worry about that yet.

For the moment my problem was getting back to the Society Cafe. I didn't see how I could sneak out of the house at midnight. That was too much of a risk.

Then it dawned on me that I didn't have to sneak out in the middle of the night. Didn't that cornet player say that sometimes they played until the sun came up? Maybe if I went over there first thing in the morning they'd still be playing. I knew I'd better do it soon, in case they stopped working there.

So the next morning I got up early, even before John was up. "My," Ma said, stirring the oatmeal on the stove. "You're an early bird this morning, Paulie."

"John was snoring." That was true—he had the sniffles.

"Well, the oatmeal isn't quite ready."

There wasn't any use in trying to get out of there without breakfast—Ma wouldn't stand for it. So I danced around from one foot to the next until she served out my bowl. I shoved the oatmeal home, gobbled down my milk, and raced out of there.

The sun hadn't come up over the buildings yet, and the streets were empty and quiet—a milk wagon clip-clopping along, a newspaper truck rumbling by with a couple of kids hanging on to the back, ready to leap off with the papers. As soon as I was out of sight of our apartment, I started to run towards the Society Cafe. It was a good distance, about twenty blocks, and by the time I got there I was panting and sweating some. I stood at the corner to get myself calmed down for a minute; then I walked down the street to the place.

It looked worse by daylight than it had at night, for you could see how rusty the tin roof was, and how much paint had scaled off the clapboards. But none of that mattered to me, for I could hear coming faintly through the door the thump of the drums and the chime of a cornet. I went up the steps, feeling pretty nervous, and knocked. Nothing happened. I swallowed, and knocked again, louder. For a minute more nothing happened, and then a small panel in the door slid open. I could see one eye and part of a nose. "Whadya want, kid?"

"My pa sent me. We left a wrench here when we were fixing the pipes last week."

"You Frankie Horvath's kid?"

"Yes." I was surprised he knew Pa's name. Mostly people just called him the plumber. "I might have left it in the toilet. Or in the cellar."

The panel slid closed. I stood there waiting, wondering if he had gone away for good. Time went along, and I was just about ready to give up, when the panel slid open again. "There ain't no wrench in the toilet."

"It must be in the cellar, then."

"Jesus," he said.

"Pa'll kill me if I don't find it."

"Okay," he said. "Go on around back. I'll let you in."

I skipped down the alley to the cellar door, and waited some more. Finally the door opened. It was the same big guy, only this time he wasn't wearing an overcoat, just a dark suit, and a white shirt buttoned up at the neck, no tie. Now I could hear the music more clear, for the trapdoor was up: piano, drums, banjo, cornet, and saxophone. The big man jerked his head towards the cellar. "Help yourself," he said. "Slam that door good when you go out." He went back up the cellar stairs, grunting through the hole in the floor and let the trapdoor slam shut.

Now what? I was happy enough just to listen to the music, and if I had the time I could have sat down there in the damp, stinky cellar all day and listened. But I had to get to school soon. I stood there for a few minutes, so as to make it seem like I was looking around for the wrench. Then I climbed up the cellar stairs and knocked on the trapdoor.

Nothing happened. I went back down the cellar stairs, found a half a brick lying on the dirt floor, went back up the stairs, and pounded on the trapdoor with the brick. Suddenly the trapdoor flung up. The big guy in the dark suit was staring down at me. "What the hell do you want now?"

"The wrench isn't down here. I figure it must be up there somewhere."

"Naw, it ain't up here. I told you, I looked in the toilet."

"Maybe I left it someplace else. Pa's going to be awful sore if I don't find it."

"It ain't like Frankie Horvath to leave tools laying around."

It sounded like he knew Pa pretty well, which surprised me. I thought he'd be just a plumber to him. "It was my fault. That's why he made me come find it myself."

He jerked his head in the general direction of the barroom. "I'll give you five minutes. Then I'm gonna run you the hell out of here."

I climbed up out of the cellar and stood up behind the bar, looking across the room to the band. There was hardly anybody in the joint—one couple dancing, another couple sitting at a table, and three men and a woman at another table, laughing. For a minute I stood there, just listening to the music, trying to figure out how they got that rocking feeling, that bounce or whatever you called it. I noticed that they had a different pianist from the one that was there before—a white guy.

I didn't have much time. I started to go around the bar, when suddenly the music stopped without any warning. In the kind of music we played at Hull House—marches, overtures, medleys of folk songs—you could tell when the end was coming. But this stuff didn't give you any warning; it just stopped.

The fellas in the band stood there by the piano for a minute. Then the cornet player laid his horn on top of the piano, and strolled towards the door with the saxophone player.

I slipped back down the cellar stairs, raced out of the cellar, slammed the door tight and ran around to the street. The two musicians were standing on the sidewalk in front of the place, shivering a little in the cold morning air. It was around seven-thirty, and every once in a while they blinked, like they weren't used to daylight. I stood a few feet away, looking at them, and trying to figure out what to say to them. Finally the cornetist noticed me. "Hello, kid," he said. "What the hell are you doing around here this time of day?"

"I came over to hear you play."

He cocked his head sideways. "You the kid with the plumber?"

"Yeah, that was me."

The saxophone wasn't paying any attention to me.

"Tommy, we got to do something about that damn banjo player. He plays like he was driving nails. He can't swing a lick."

Under my breath I said, "Tommy," just to try it out.

"He's all right," Tommy said. "He's doing the best he can."

"That's the trouble," the saxophone said. "If he wasn't doing the best he could we could improve him. But as it is, we can't."

"He thinks he's doing all right," Tommy said. "I haven't got the heart to say nothing to him."

I would have liked to have stood there awhile, just listening to them talk. It was like they had a secret club that maybe I could get into. But they were bound to go back inside pretty soon. I walked closer. "Could I ask you something?"

The saxophone put on a kind of disgusted look, but Tommy said, "Sure, kid."

"I play cornet in the Hull House band. How could I learn to play like you do?"

"You're at Hull House? Benny Goodman came out of there. And Art Hodes. How long you been at Hull House?"

I heard of both of those guys. Benny Goodman was supposed to be some kind of genius. He wasn't more than a couple of years older than me, but already he was playing professionally and making a pile of dough. Art Hodes was a piano player. He was older and played in a dance band they had at Hull

House called the Marionettes. "I started there in the summer," I said.

"That's the first you played cornet?"

I didn't want to seem like too much of a beginner. "I studied piano for a while, too."

"It's plain to see the kid's a boy genius," the saxophone said. He flapped his arms to warm up. "We better go in, Tommy, before Herbie has kittens."

"We got a couple of minutes," Tommy said. "We played six sets already. What does Herbie want, for God's sake?"

"Listen," I said quickly, looking at Tommy. "I wonder if you could give me lessons." I didn't have any idea how I would pay him.

Tommy laughed. "That ain't exactly my line. I don't know how I do it myself. You got to get a feeling for it."

"Come on, Tommy, let's go in," the saxophone said. "I'm freezing out here."

"Maybe you could just show me stuff."

"He told you no once," the saxophone said. "Come on, Tommy."

"You're real eager, ain't you, kid. What's your name?"

"Paulie Horvath. My Pa's Frankie Horvath."

He reached into his hip pocket, took out a worn-out wallet, and poked around inside of it. "Here," he said finally. He handed me a dirty card that had been bent in half at least once and straightened out. "You might catch me at home around five or six sometime. We got to go back on."

They turned and went on back up the steps to the Society Cafe. I stood there looking at the card in my hand:

TOMMY HURD AND HIS JOYMAKERS.
MUSIC FOR ALL OCCASIONS.

It felt like somebody had given me a key to a room where there was a store of gold and jewels, if only I could get to that door. Tommy's address was out in the near South Side somewhere. It'd be a hike to get down there, but I could walk it.

5 THE NEXT MORNING I got up late as usual, flung on my clothes, and raced out to the kitchen, where my oatmeal in my yellow bowl was on the kitchen table, stone cold, with a crust on top. I dumped some cream and sugar on it, stirred it around to mix the crust in, and gulped it down.

Ma came in. "Paulie, that shirt's filthy. Take it off this instant." I'd got dirt on it from prowling around in that barroom cellar.

"I'm late, Ma."

"You're not going to school in that shirt. What'll your teachers think?" And while I was sitting there gulping away at my oatmeal, she began to unbutton it down my front.

"I'll do it, Ma," I said. I jumped up from the table,

flung off the shirt, ran into our room to grab another shirt, put on my jacket, and tore out of there. And it wasn't until I was standing by my desk in my home-room mumbling the Pledge of Allegiance that I remembered that Tommy Hurd's bent card was in that shirt pocket.

I ran all the way home after school. Ma was standing over the ironing board in the kitchen. Beside her was her clothes basket, and on the kitchen table a stack of neatly folded stuff she'd ironed. My shirt was there in the stack. I pulled it out, and stuck my hand in the breast pocket.

Ma was watching me. "I threw it away, Paulie."

"Ma."

"Where did you get it?"

To be honest, I didn't believe in lying. If you felt a certain way, why shouldn't you be honest about it? I mean, no matter what anybody said, you ought to be able to tell the truth. But sometimes you couldn't, that was plain. "Some kid at Hull House gave it to me."

"It's some sort of cheap jazz band, isn't it?"

"Ma, there's nothing wrong with jazz."

"What were you planning to do?"

"I figured I might take lessons from him."

"You're already taking from Mr. Sylvester," she said. "That's plenty. You've got your schoolwork to consider."

"Where did you throw it? I'm going to find it."

"I tore it up and flushed it down the toilet."

"Ma," I shouted. "It was mine."

"Paulie, it's one thing to play in the Hull House band, where they've got proper supervision. But I'm not having you getting mixed up with a lot of low-class jazz musicians. That's flat."

But it didn't matter what she said—I *was* going to get involved with a lot of low-class jazz musicians. I hated going against her. Me and Ma usually got on pretty good, for she made allowances about me not being like everybody else, which Pa didn't. But she could only make allowances so far, and then the fringed lampshades got in the way. It made me sad to think that we had to disagree. I went around feeling disloyal, like I'd broken my word to her, and sometimes when she started to joke around with me, I felt bad, and couldn't get into it the way I used to. But what could I do about it?

Two days later I was sitting on my bed in our room, puffing away at the cornet, trying to get that rocking feeling that Tommy Hurd put into his music. John was sitting at the table, doing his homework. Suddenly he raised up his head. "Shut up a minute, Paulie, I want to hear."

"What?"

"Shhhh." We sat quiet. Somebody was talking in a big, heavy voice.

"Come on outside, Frankie. We got to have a little chat." There was something familiar about the voice, but I couldn't catch it.

Pa's voice came through the bedroom door. "We can chat here, Herbie."

Herbie. Was it that big guy from the Society Cafe?

"I got a couple of things I wouldn't want to say in front of your old lady. You better come out with us."

Then Ma's voice came: "What's it about, Frank?"

"I don't know. It's some kind of mistake. I'll go straighten it out."

"Let's hope it's some kind of mistake, Frankie," Herbie said.

For a minute there was nothing, and then we heard the front door shut. The next minute our bedroom door opened and Ma put her head in. "Pa had to go out on business," she said. "Supper'll be a little late. You boys just go on with what you're doing." She shut the door.

I sat there holding the cornet on my lap, feeling mighty worried. Did it have anything to do with me? Did he come over to tell Pa I was over there? "What do you think it is, John? Why wouldn't he talk with Pa in the apartment?"

"I don't know," he said. "Maybe it's nothing. Maybe they just had to talk to Pa about something."

It wasn't about nothing—that much I knew. It was about something, and it scared me. I didn't feel like playing, so I picked up John's copy of *The Wampus Cat* and lay on the bed trying to read. But I couldn't concentrate on reading, either, so I just lay there, worrying, and listening to John's pen scratch along the paper as he worked on his history report.

Finally we heard the apartment door open. John

stopped scratching. We heard Ma say, "Frank, what did they do to you? Are you all right?"

"I'm all right. They just crowded me a little."

"What was it all about?"

"That's just what I'm going to find out."

It was me. I sat up on the bed listening to his footsteps come closer. The door swung open. Pa stood there, looking at me. His eye was swollen and there was a scratch down his cheek.

Suddenly I wished I'd planned things out a little more. It was one thing to sneak off to the Society Cafe to hear those guys play. It was another thing to get Pa smacked around for it. I felt mighty sick in the pit of my stomach. I wished I hadn't done it. I wished I'd thought about it more before I ran over there. But it was too late for wishing.

"John," Pa said without taking his eyes off me, "Go somewhere else. I got to talk to Paulie." He went on looking at me. "Close the door behind you."

"Pa—" But I couldn't think of anything to say.

"What was you doing in that joint the other morning?"

I was plenty scared. "I wasn't doing anything wrong, Pa."

"That's for me to decide. What was you doing there? You told them I sent you to find a wrench. I never sent you there."

I hung my head down. "I went to hear those guys play," I whispered.

"Look at me." I put my head up. "What the hell

did you need to hear them for? You got a whole band of your own over at Hull House."

"It isn't the same. It's a different kind of music."

"I know what it is, Paulie. It's that nigger music."

"Those guys are white," I said.

"That don't make no difference. It makes me sick to see all these white people running after that nigger music. I don't want you to have anything to do with it. And if I ever hear of you going anywheres near that joint again I'm going to beat you within an inch of your life." Then before I knew it, he whacked me good and hard across my face with the back of his hand. It snapped my head back and for a moment I went blank. I felt myself sway, but I didn't fall. "That's just to remind you I'm serious," he said. He turned and walked out of the room.

I sat down on the bed. I knew he was serious all right, for it was the first time he ever hit me like that. Spanked me a few times when I was little, but never hit me before. The tears were trying to force themselves out of my eyes. I squeezed my whole face up tight. The tears leaked out anyway, but at least I didn't make any noise. Finally I took one long, wavery breath in and got control of myself. And a minute later Ma came in and said, "Come on out now and eat supper, Paulie."

GETTING PA IN trouble, especially with gangsters, made me feel mighty low and quiet, not much like practicing. What had happened? What was it all about? The whole thing seemed so unfair. All I wanted to do was to learn how to play jazz, and here was Pa getting beat up for it. Suppose every time I tried to find out about jazz something like this happened. What was fair about that? How come they knew who Pa was? How come they knew where we lived? Did Ma know anything about it? There wasn't any use in asking her, for she'd just tell me it wasn't any of my business and to stay out of it.

Anyway, the whole thing made me feel kind of quiet, and for a while I laid low, and came right home from school instead of going over to Rory's. I even did some homework for a change, and got an eighty on an English test.

But in a few days I began to perk up and think about jazz again. I saw right away that records were the answer. I didn't know anything about records—how much they cost, or even if there was such a thing as jazz records. One problem was, I didn't have any money, what with always getting my allowance docked. But I figured I could get some money off John. He always had plenty, from doing his chores and working for Pa on Saturdays. So the next afternoon I went over to the music counter at the five-and-dime and asked the guy if he heard of any jazz records.

"Jazz records? I got a slew of 'em. How come a smart kid like you didn't know that?"

"I'm not too smart," I said. "I'm not doing so hot in school."

"That explains it, then," he said. "I tell you, I got all the greatest jazz records right here—New Orleans Rhythm Kings, Louisiana Five, Original Dixieland Jazz Band. You name it, I got it."

"Which is best?"

"Well five years ago the Original Dixieland Jazz Band was all the rage. They sold millions. They came up from New Orleans to Chi, along with Brown's Band from Dixieland. That's where they got famous, right here in Chicago. They didn't have anything of that kind of music in New York then. But them bands are kind of old hat now. If you want to know my opinion, right now the best is the New Orleans Rhythm Kings. And I'll tell you why I recommend them." He gave me a serious look. "You want to know why?"

"Sure."

"It's because they're playing right here in Chicago out on the North Side at the Friars' Inn. I've been out there a dozen times myself. You could say I practically live there. The fellas in the band all know me. They got this here clarinet player who's the cat's pajamas. Leon Roppolo is his name, but they all call him Rop. Oh, the Rhythm Kings are the best. Why they haven't got anything in New York that's even a patch on them." He frowned. "Of course, that's not counting the colored bands."

I wanted to ask him if he thought jazz was nigger music, but I was afraid he might take it wrong. So instead I said, "Are there a lot of colored bands, or what?"

"Go over to the South Side, you won't hear anything *but* colored bands. King Oliver, Lawrence Duhé, all of them."

"Are they better than the white bands?"

"Oh, they got some mighty good bands, those colored. King Oliver, he's no slouch. They got a natural feeling for it, you know. Born with it. But Oliver and them didn't make any records yet."

"But the whites can play jazz, too, can't they?"

"You bet they can. The Rhythm Kings, they're the cat's pajamas."

"Have you got their records?"

"You wouldn't ask a question like that if you was smarter. Of course I got 'em."

"How much are they?"

"Seventy-five cents and worth twice that. At least twice that."

"Oh," I said. "I don't have that much. I guess I'll have to save up."

"You should. You'll never regret it."

I went on home. John was in our room finishing off his history report. "Hey, John," I said, "How about loaning me seventy-five cents?"

"Come off it, Paulie. How'd you ever pay me back? I'll be an old man before you see any allowance again."

"I'll do all the dishes for a month."

He gave me a squinty look, just like Ma. "What do you need seventy-five cents for?"

"You look like Ma when you do that."

He laid off the squinty look. "What's the money for?"

Usually I would have told him. But suddenly I decided not to. He wouldn't squeal on his brother. But even so, he was basically on their side and might forget himself and let something slip out. "Just something," I said.

"Don't give me that," he said. "I'm not going to loan you some money if I don't know what it's for."

"Why do you have to know? It isn't any of your business."

"I'm making it my business," he said. "Suppose you were planning on buying a gun or something."

"How could you buy a gun for seventy-five cents?"

"I didn't say you were. That was just an example."

I began to see that I'd have to tell him; but before I could blurt anything out he said, "It's for a girl, isn't it, Paulie? You're stuck on some girl and you want to take her to a dance and buy her a soda afterwards."

That was luck. I tried to make myself blush. "No, it isn't for any girl."

"Who is she?" he said. "Mary Hartwell?"

"I said it wasn't any girl, John."

"Agnes Fincke? Helen whatshername with the long pigtail? I'll bet it's her."

"I don't even know who you mean," which wasn't true. Helen Schein was getting pretty cute.

"All right," he said. "But you got to do all the dishes for a month. And pick up your clothes around here so I don't keep tripping on them."

A month was an awful long time. But I knew better than to argue with him. "I promise," I said. I figured I could get out of it someway after a couple of weeks, anyway.

"And you better pay me back."

Both of us knew there wasn't the slightest chance of that, not until we were grown-ups. "Okay," I said.

I wanted to rush out right away and buy a jazz record, but I couldn't, because John would get suspicious. Oh, I could hardly stand waiting—I couldn't think of anything else all evening, and I might as well not have gone to school the next day, for all I learned. What if it turned out that the New Orleans Rhythm Kings record wasn't any good? Suppose it didn't give me that feeling that Tommy Hurd's band did? Suppose it was just plain music? I didn't see how that guy at the five-and-dime could be wrong, though. But suppose he was?

I didn't wait a minute after the last bell rang, but grabbed Rory and off we went to the five-and-dime. The same guy was there. "Well if it isn't the jazzbo kid. Got hold of some money, did you?"

"I borrowed it off my brother."

He looked at Rory. "You having trouble at school, too?"

"Hell, I got left back."

"I'm shocked," the guy said. He took a record off the shelf, and handed it to me. It was the New Orleans Rhythm Kings. One side was "Oriental" and the other "Farewell Blues." "I'm recommending this one," the guy said. "It's the cat's meow."

"I thought it was the cat's pajamas."

He gave me a look. "You got a pretty smart tongue for a kid who isn't doing so hot in school."

I didn't want to argue with him, but I gave him the money and we walked back to Rory's, me holding on to that record with two hands and walking slow so I wouldn't trip. It was a thrill just to have that record in my hands. In my whole life I never owned anything that gave me such a thrill—not the fielder's mitt Pa got me for my tenth birthday, not even when I got my cornet from Hull House.

Rory's apartment was on the third floor—just a kitchen, and two other rooms with a bed in each, a table, a couple of chairs. Rory had cut out pictures of guys from the Cubs and stuck them on his walls, and Mrs. Flynn had put up a few ads from magazines in the other room. There was a calendar in the kitchen, but it was two years old and was there for the pictures, which Mrs. Flynn changed around from time to time, so that even the right month wasn't up.

They didn't have a toilet up there—you had to go down to an outhouse in the backyard. The phonograph was in the room where Mrs. Flynn usually slept. Some old boyfriend of hers had given it to her a long time before. It was pretty beat up—the box all scratched and the handle loose, so you had to hold it at a certain angle when you wound it up. I tell you, my hand actually trembled when I slipped that record over the spindle. Rory wound it up good and tight. I pushed the lever to set it spinning, and put the needle on. Out came the music.

Well, it was something, all right. I stood there with my mouth open, just hypnotized. Of course it was sort of tinny, nothing like as clear and alive as the real thing. But it had that magic to it, that bounce, that sparkle, and it made me sparkle inside, too.

"What the hell kind of music is that?" Rory said.

"Shhhh," I said. Rory sat down and began tapping his foot to it, but I went on standing, not able to move.

Finally the record got done. "Boy, isn't that something," I said.

"I didn't get it," Rory said. "It sounded pretty confused."

"You got to get used to it." I turned the record over and played the other side, standing as close as I could to the phonograph so as to hear it as good as I could. Then I turned it back to the first side and listened to it all over again.

"How many times you going to play that damn thing?" Rory said.

"I don't know. A lot."

"I don't know if I can stand it, Horvath."

"You'll get used to it," I said.

6   I COULDN'T LET that New Orleans Rhythm Kings record alone. I hated leaving it at Rory's house for fear of it getting busted—they weren't too careful about things around there. But I didn't have anyplace to hide it at home. Ma was always going into our room for some reason or other—put away clean clothes after she washed them, or pick up my mess when she couldn't stand it anymore. There was no telling when she might decide to air out our beds or clean out our closet; it was too risky to hide anything there.

So I left the record at Rory's, and every afternoon I went there and played it over and over. Finally Rory said he couldn't take it anymore, he was being driven out of house and home. So I started playing it at Hull House in the room where they had dancing class. Most of the time nobody was there. And about the second day I was playing it there I got the idea of trying to play my cornet along with it. I took a straight mute out of the closet in the band room—the closet was supposed to be locked, but you could open it if you twisted the knob real hard. I picked "Farewell Blues" to start with. With the mute in I was able to hear the record over my playing. It didn't take me but a minute to realize I was out of tune with the music. But there was a knob on the phonograph which you could turn to speed the turntable up or slow it down, and by fooling around a little I got myself in tune. Then I tried this note and that note until I got a few that fit in here and there. It was funny, though: I'd find a note that fit in pretty good, and then it would go sour. What was that about? It seemed like they were changing keys or something. I decided the best thing to do was to copy off exactly what the cornetist was playing.

It was mighty hard. I'd play the first couple of measures of the record and try to get it on my horn. It was a struggle, and by the time a half hour was up I was pretty discouraged and ready to give it up. But I stuck to it, and after a while I saw that if I learned to sing what the cornetist was playing, I had an easier time of getting it on my horn. So I kept on banging away, and after an hour, when my lip was red and sore, I'd got a chunk of it—the whole first eight bars, except for a couple of spots here and there where it seemed like he was playing in between the notes or something.

That was the way it went. Every afternoon I'd go over to Hull House and bang away at "Farewell Blues" until after a few days somebody came out of the director's office and told me that much as they appreciated my love for music, I was driving the staff crazy and I had to give them a rest for a while. I started taking the record and my cornet to Rory's until he couldn't stand it either, and then I snuck back into Hull House.

By this time I could see that I could learn stuff off records, if I stuck with it. I also could see that if I learned "Oriental" and "Farewell Blues," it might be enough to persuade Tommy Hurd to teach me, if I could ever find him again. So I buckled down to it every day.

Then at night I'd have my regular practicing to do for Mr. Sylvester—exercises from the Arban book, *Clarke's Method for Cornet*, the songbook. My lip was sore half the time. And naturally, I didn't do a lick of homework, from one week to the next. Before, I'd always managed to get just enough done so I'd pass. I knew it would worry Ma something dreadful if I got left back, and somehow, when danger threatened, I'd pull and haul myself through.

But that was before, when I didn't have anything else I was interested in, and might as well study instead of sitting around reading John's old *Wampus Cat* I'd read six times already. Now homework was in the way of practicing. Oh, I knew it was going to be nothing but trouble if I flunked. Pa would raise hell and Ma would go around looking worried. It would be smarter to do a little homework now and again. But I couldn't make myself do it. I'd promise myself I was just going to practice for an hour, and then do my history or whatever it was. But, of course, I'd run over the hour by fifteen minutes; and tell myself I might as well make it an hour and a half, so as to have it come out even. Then I'd put the cornet down, pick up my history book, and about two minutes later I'd remember something I wanted to try on the cornet, which wouldn't take more than a couple of minutes; and the next thing I knew Ma had poked her head in our bedroom, saying it was time for bed.

Of course Ma noticed—she couldn't help but notice with me banging away at the horn all the time. She'd come into our room and say, "I hope you've done your homework, Paulie," or something like that. I'd say, "I'm going to do it in a minute." She'd say, "Just remember, Paulie, if you don't do good in school, no more cornet." So I'd promise myself I really would start doing my homework. But the next day it'd be the same thing all over again. The shame of it was that Ma and Pa wouldn't give me any credit for working hard at music. To them, that didn't count; to me, doing good in school and rising up in the world didn't count.

But Ma had other things on her mind besides my

schoolwork. Grampa Horvath had taken sick. It didn't look too good and Ma had to keep going out to take care of him. Pa's brothers and sisters all lived downstate or out in California and couldn't be much use. So it was left to Ma.

After about two weeks of working on that record I'd pretty much got both sides of it down, and was trying to figure out a way to get another record, for I knew that John wouldn't give me any more money. Then one day when I came in for my lesson, I noticed Mr. Sylvester staring at me close. "What have you been doing to yourself, Horvath?"

"What do you mean?"

"You look like somebody popped you in the mouth."

I rubbed my lip. "Yeah, I've been practicing a lot recent."

"I'll say you have. How much are you playing a day? A couple hours?"

"More, I guess," I said.

"How much?"

"Well, generally a couple of hours in the afternoon."

"And?"

"A couple of more hours after supper."

"My God," he said. He grabbed hold of my chin and took a close look at my lips. Then he let go and pointed to some music on the stand. "Play that." I played a few bars. He sat bent forward, watching my mouth. "Okay, that's enough." He leaned back and crossed his arms over his chest. "What made you get serious about music all of a sudden, Horvath? Up till now you weren't my worst student, but you weren't my best by a long shot, either."

I didn't want to mention about the jazz. "I decided to be a musician. Somebody was telling me about this kid Benny Goodman who used to go here. He's already making good money."

"Well, sure, but Benny's something special. They don't come along like him very often. I'm not going to say you couldn't be pretty good if you worked at it, I wouldn't even guess about that. But you shouldn't expect to be a hotshot like Benny right away."

"I can try, though."

He uncrossed his arms and took hold of my chin again, turning my face this way and that so as to get a good look at my mouth. "Well," he said, "If you're really serious, we'll have to start over again."

"What?" My heart sank.

"For one thing, you're developing a roll. You can split your lip that way. For another, you're using too much pressure. Feel your teeth—I'll bet they're already getting loose."

I grabbed hold of my upper front teeth and wiggled them. He was right; they moved just a little.

"How high have you been playing?"

Of course I'd been going up to wherever that cornetist on the Rhythm Kings took me. "I can make an A pretty easy. Sometimes a C."

He shook his head. "Nope. We've got to start over again."

"You mean you were teaching me wrong all along?"

"Horvath, be sensible. I got thirty kids, I can't baby all of them along. Anytime I see a kid who's serious, I'll work with him. But you couldn't make most of these little dears into musicians if you were a fairy godmother with a magic wand. They're only interested in marching around in those uniforms. You were all right the way you were going so long as you were like the rest of them—practice half an hour a day at best, rehearse once a week, play six concerts a year. On that schedule you couldn't hurt yourself no matter what you were doing wrong. But four hours a day—that's another story."

I hung my head down. I felt just sunk. All that work for nothing. The whole thing had been a waste. I looked up at him. "How long will it take?"

"Six months and we'll have you in some kind of shape."

"Six months?" It sounded like forever.

He laughed. "You'll live," he said. "You'll come out ahead in the end. We'll give you a nice firm embouchure, good intonation, some range without all that pressure."

There was no way around it. I could see that he was right. My lips had a nice red ring around them all the time. Either I had to quit or do what he told me to do.

Oh, but it was awful. At first he had me playing nothing but long tones: start down at the bottom on F-sharp and work my way up, holding each note out until I ran out of breath, all the while trying to keep the pitch centered. I was so used to digging the mouthpiece into my lip, the first couple of days without pressure I could hardly get a tone out. But it began to come along, and pretty soon I could see some progress. Before, when I hit a note, it was likely to be a little off at the first instant—flat or sharp or rough or choked—until I pulled it to where it was supposed to be. The ordinary person wouldn't notice exactly what was wrong, but they'd know it was some kid playing. Now I was beginning to hit the notes right on the nose. Seeing some progress cheered me up a good deal, for I knew that in the long run I was going to be way ahead of the other kids in the band. I knew what they were doing wrong, and I wasn't doing it anymore.

Of course it meant I had to give up playing jazz for a while. I'd just ruin myself all over again if I went back to "Farewell Blues," and there wasn't any point in going out to look for Tommy Hurd; I couldn't play for him. All I could do was be patient and slog away every day: it'd come, Mr. Sylvester said.

In the meantime, I couldn't play in the band. The big joke about that was at Thanksgiving they marched in a parade, and of course I was out of it and didn't get to wear a uniform. But by Christmastime I'd got enough of a lip worked up so I could get back into the band on third cornet, where I wouldn't have a lot of high notes. I played the Hull House Christmas concert, and finally got to put on one of those fancy uniforms. It didn't mean anything to me anymore. The way I felt about music, what difference did it make what I was wearing when I played it? I could be in my pajamas for all it mattered.

So the weeks went along. Day by day I built my lip up. Mr. Sylvester was right: I just had to be patient and keep after it. I was hitting the notes nice and clean, with a full sound, and I could see the time would come when I'd make high C's without any trouble.

In March my birthday came, and I turned thirteen. What I wanted for my birthday was a Harmon mute, but there wasn't any chance I'd get one, for Ma believed in practical presents. I got a winter coat and a winter hat with earflaps, even though winter was almost over; winter clothes were on sale that time of year, and Ma got the coat a little big, so I could grow into it. We had cake and ice cream and when they sang "Happy Birthday" to me I got out my cornet and played it along with them.

Pa gave me a couple of days to get used to being thirteen and then over supper he sprung it on me. "Paulie's thirteen. It's time he done something useful around here."

"Did," Ma said.

"Done or did, so long as he does it. I'm going to start him off working with me regular."

"I don't want Paulie taking time away from school," Ma said. "He mustn't get left back."

"What time off school?" Pa said. "He hasn't done a lick of homework for weeks that I saw. He spent all his time playing that damn cornet."

"I did *some* homework."

"Frank, you got to admit that Paulie's worked hard at his music. He's stuck to it."

"That's the problem. It's just like Paulie to stick at something you can't make a living at. If I knew he was going to stick at it I wouldn't of let him start in the first place. I figured it'd be like everything else he put his hand to—here today and gone tomorrow."

The whole thing was making me mighty nervous. He'd make me work with him Saturdays for sure. What if he made me work after school, too? My embouchure was coming along real good: I couldn't quit now. I wished I could persuade them. "You can make a living being a musician," I said. "Did you ever hear of this kid Benny Goodman? He was at Hull House last year. He's making big money and he's only fourteen or something."

Pa rapped his knuckles on the table. "Paulie, I don't want to hear no more about being a musician."

"Any more," Ma said.

"Any more, no more. John started working with me when he was twelve. He kept up his schoolwork good, too."

The upshot of it was that on Saturday morning Pa rousted me out of bed at six-thirty, and by seven me and him and John were on the streetcar with the toolboxes headed out to the West Side. "What kind of a place is it, Pa?"

Pa looked around at the people on the streetcar. Then he said, "You'll see soon enough."

We got out there. It was a neighborhood mostly of two-story brick houses. Smack in the middle of the block was a row of stores, and upstairs over them a dance hall. Lettered along the windows was PEA-COCK BALLROOM. We walked along, and then when we were about a hundred feet from the place, Pa stopped. He bent forward, so as to get his face close to mine. "Now, Paulie," he said in a low voice. "This here is another one of Herbie Aronowitz's joints. I don't want you getting into no foolishness like you did before. You understand, son?"

"Pa, is Herbie a gang—"

Before I could finish Pa had reached out and given me a shake. "That's the exact thing I meant. You go in there, you do your job, you don't see nothing, and you don't talk about nothing but the Cubs." He gave me a steady look and squeezed my shoulder a little. "You got me, son?"

"Yes, Pa."

I wasn't sure I liked the idea of Pa working for a gangster. Some people admired gangsters and would boast about how they knew Al Capone's second cousin, or had come along two days after some gangster got machine-gunned and saw the red spot where he'd bled to death on the sidewalk. And I could see how you could get excited by getting to know one. But there was something about them I didn't like—that kind of badness to them, blood and death and slamming people around because they didn't like your face. Of course, all I really knew about gangsters was what it said in the newspapers: how they beat up some old Chink laundryman because he didn't pay protection money, or got into a gang war over control of the gambling joints. According to the papers, the gangsters ran Chicago, and the government was in cahoots with them. Pa always said you couldn't believe anything you read in the papers, but I wasn't so sure. Some of it had to be right, and it seemed clear enough to me that gangsters weren't very nice in general. So why would Pa want to have anything to do with them? I wished I understood it. I figured I'd ask John when I got a chance.

But I couldn't ask anything then. We marched on up the street, went through a door with PEACOCK BALLROOM lettered on it in swirly gold letters that had got worn and scratched, and up a flight of stairs to the dance hall. There was a bandstand down at one end of the room and a bar at the other, and along the walls small tables and wire chairs. On the bandstand there was an old upright piano, and on the wall behind the piano a banner saying TOMMY HURD AND HIS JOYMAKERS.

Just to see that sign set my heart thumping. Tommy had been on my mind so much for so long I wasn't sure he was real anymore, that the whole thing at the Society Cafe had really happened. But here he was, real again at last.

When I thought about it, though, I could see it wasn't awful surprising for me to run into him again. Pa worked for Herbie Aronowitz and so did Tommy—why wouldn't we bump into each other from time to time? The big question was whether I would get a chance to talk to him.

Did Pa remember that Tommy was the guy from the Society Cafe? Probably he wouldn't; it wasn't like Pa to stick something in his mind that didn't have to do with work and rising up in the world. And if Tommy came in while we were there, what would Pa say if I went over and talked to him?

But I couldn't think about it then, for we had work to do. They were putting in tap beer, and our job was to run pipes up from the cellar where they kept the beer kegs. Pa sent John down to the cellar, and after that it was, "Paulie, hand me that there pipe wrench." "Paulie, see if you can find a one-inch T in the box." "Paulie, for God's sake hold the damn pipe steady." Of course, being as it was Prohibition, it was illegal to sell beer. And it crossed my mind that maybe it was illegal to put in a tap set-up, too. It made me feel kind of funny that Pa might be breaking the law.

Anyway, I was mainly thinking about whether I'd run across Tommy Hurd. "Pa, what time do you figure we'll get finished this afternoon?"

He had a carpenter's pencil in his mouth. "We got to be out of here by five. They open up at six."

There was the answer: they didn't want plumbers working in there when the band was playing and the customers dancing. Still, maybe Tommy'd come in early to warm up. But the day went on, and by four o'clock we'd got the job pretty much done. Pa told me to find a broom and sweep up where we'd been drilling and sawing. There was a little kitchen behind the bar, where an old man with big yellow teeth like a horse was making sandwiches. "You got a broom anywhere?" I asked.

He pointed over his shoulder with the bread knife. "In that there closet, sonny."

I opened the closet door. It was filled with junk—shelves along the back heaped up with cans of nails, rolls of string, boxes of candles, a couple of oil lamps, and a dustpan. Hanging from a hook was a dirty apron. A mop bucket sat on the floor and a couple of brooms leaned up against the shelves. I grabbed the dustpan. A pad of notepaper came up with it and dropped to the floor. I picked it up and started to put it back on the shelf, when suddenly an idea came into my mind. It wasn't an idea Pa would like very much, but I was getting to the place where I didn't much care what he thought. I ripped a sheet of paper off the pad, and stuck it in my back pocket. Then I snatched up the broom and dustpan, went back out into the barroom and began to sweep up.

Pa was crouched down behind the bar with the

flashlight, checking the new pipe joints for leaks. I swept my way over to the toolbox, knelt down like I was sweeping stuff into the dustpan, and rambled around in the tools until I found a carpenter's pencil. I put the sheet of notepaper on the floor, and wrote:

Dear Tommy Hurd,

I lost your card. Please send me your address again so I can take cornet from you.

Your pal,
Paulie Horvath. The plumber's boy.
1635 West Seventeenth Street.

I folded the paper, stood up, picked up the broom and swept my way across the ballroom to the bandstand. When I got there I looked back. Pa was out of sight down behind the bar. I slipped up onto the bandstand and eased the front of the piano open, trying not to make any noise. When I'd got it lifted up about a foot I gently pushed down middle C, a note any pianist was bound to play almost as soon as he sat down, just enough to raise the hammer. That told me which were the C strings. I stuck the note in between two of the strings: when the pianist hit middle C he'd get nothing but a dead clunk. He was bound to open the piano to see what the trouble was. I pushed the piano closed again, but of course my hand slipped and half an octave fired off like a gong. Pa popped up from behind the bar.

"What're you doing with that piano, Paulie?"

"There was some sawdust on the keys, Pa. I was just dusting it off."

"Never mind about that. Go get John and let's get out of here."

7   A COUPLE OF days went by, and then a week, and I didn't hear anything from Tommy Hurd. It was hard to know what might have happened. Maybe he didn't get the note; maybe the piano player just pulled it out of the strings and threw it away without looking at it. I wished I'd written something on the outside of it, like *Please don't throw away*, or something. Or maybe Tommy didn't want to be bothered with teaching some kid in the first place. But if that was so, why did he give me the card? Or maybe Herbie got into it and told Tommy not to have anything to do with me. I didn't know what had happened, but I didn't hear anything from Tommy.

By this time my lip had come along good enough

so I was back to playing with that Rhythm Kings record. I knew my instrument a whole lot better than I'd done before, and it was a lot easier for me to pick up from the record what that cornet player was doing. I could see that it was just like everything else; if I kept after it, copying stuff off records would get easier and easier. But I only had that one jazz record and didn't know how I was ever going to get any more. I couldn't borrow from John again—there wasn't any hope of that. I figured that if I went on working with Pa on plumbing jobs, sooner or later he'd ease up on docking my allowance and give me a little money here and there. But knowing Pa, he wasn't going to be in any rush about it.

Then, a couple of weeks after I'd left that note in the piano, Pa had to work late. He came in around eight. Ma fixed him his supper and he sat down to it. When he'd got it shoveled home he called me out of our room where I was practicing the Arban book, and told me to sit down opposite him at the table. Ma was at the sink, washing Pa's supper dishes.

"Why am I in trouble now, Pa?" I said.

"I don't know as you are," he said. "I was back there at that dance hall again. The band was playing and when they took a break one of those fellas came over to me."

"Tommy Hurd? Was it Tommy?"

Pa reached into his shirt pocket, took out a card and looked at it. "That's what it says here." He put the card back in the shirt pocket. "He said you left a note for him, but he didn't get around to answering it." He leaned back and looked at me. "What was you doing, writing notes to musicians?"

Ma turned around from the sink. "Paulie, that's not the same one who gave you his card before?"

Why did they have to be so against the only thing I ever really wanted? It made me feel hopeless. Wasn't there any way to convince them? "I only wanted to take lessons from him. Don't you want me to get better?"

"I don't want you playing that cheap jazz," Ma said.

There just had to be something I could say to convince them. "Jazz is very big nowadays. If I got good enough I could make a lot of dough."

That caught Pa's attention. "What kind of money you talking about?"

"The guys over at Hull House say this kid Benny Goodman makes a hundred dollars a week."

"I don't believe it," Pa said. "Who'd be crazy enough to pay a kid that kind of dough to play music?"

"That's what everybody over at Hull House says." To be honest, it was hard for me to believe, too, but everybody said it.

Pa took the card out of his pocket and tapped it on his thumbnail. "How come you need lessons from this guy? You're already getting free lessons over at Hull House."

Maybe I had a chance to convince Pa. "That's band

music. You can't make any money from band music. You got to play for dances. That's where the big money is. That's what I got to learn."

Pa tapped the card on his thumbnail again. "I don't know. I'm suspicious of it. It don't make any sense to me that you could make that kind of dough out of music."

"Frank, I don't want any child of mine working in some low-class dive."

"If I promised not to play in any dives? If I just played tea dances and excursion boats?"

"I got to think about it, Paulie," Pa said. He put the card back in his shirt pocket again. He was interested. Pa was always telling us how he had to drop out of school at twelve and go to work. He knew the value of a dollar. He wanted us to get our education, that was true; it was helpful in rising up in the world. But he said he'd never had much schooling and couldn't see where it had hurt him much. Pa wasn't as worried about low-class dives as Ma was; he'd come up rough.

But it wasn't anything I could count on. He might decide to let me take lessons from Tommy, but it was more likely he wouldn't. Ma was bound to be against it. She was pleased I'd stuck to my music, but there wasn't any hope that she'd let me go into jazz if she could help it.

Then Pa said he was tired and had to get up early. He took off his shirt, hung it over his chair, and began to wash up at the kitchen sink. Ma took down her sewing basket from the shelf and went out into the living room. I had just about one minute to slip that card out of Pa's shirt pocket, before he'd finish washing, and take the shirt into their bedroom with him. It was mighty scary to think of taking something out of Pa's pocket, even though I wasn't going to steal it, just look at it. I'd never done anything like it before.

But what else could I do? I might never get a chance like this again. I snatched the card out of Pa's shirt, took a look at it, and dropped it back into his pocket again. Then I went into our room and scribbled Tommy's address down on a piece of paper. For a minute I stood there looking down at that address. What would it be like to have parents who liked jazz, who would let me study with Tommy Hurd, and give me New Orleans Rhythm Kings records for my birthday? I figured I'd never know.

The next day I took my cornet and slipped out of the house while Ma was out shopping. It was a good long walk down to where Tommy Hurd lived. I went along as brisk as I could. I hoped people would notice me going along with the cornet. I hoped they were thinking, Look at that kid, a musician already at his age. He must be a genius. But maybe they weren't.

I found the address. It was a beat-up wooden rooming house on Twenty-fourth Street, three stories high, with a rickety porch across the front. I went up the steps to the porch. One of Tommy's cards was stuck to the doorjamb with a thumbtack. Penciled on it was SECOND FLOOR, ROOM 4. I pushed the door open. Ahead of me was a flight of stairs. The carpet on them was worn right through to the wood in places. I went up. There wasn't much light up there, but there was enough to see the yellow stains on the wallpaper and the layer of dirt on the window down at the end of the hall. I found Tommy's door and stood in front of it, feeling nervous. Suppose he got sore at me for coming over there? Maybe he didn't really want some kid bothering him.

I knocked, kind of soft. Nothing happened. Maybe he wasn't at home. I gave him a little time and knocked again, this time louder. After a minute there came a scratchy voice. "Who's there?"

"It's me. Paulie Horvath."

"Who?"

"Paulie Horvath. You gave Pa your card for me. The plumber."

For a moment there wasn't any sound. Then he said, "Oh, yeah. Come on in."

I pushed the door open and looked in. Tommy was in bed with the blanket up to his chin. His room was a worse mess than mine. His clothes were flopped over a chair, not even hung there, but just heaved there. A phonograph sat on the floor, with a lot of records scattered around it in little stacks. On the bureau was another stack of records, his beat-up wallet, a couple of crumpled dollar bills and a half-empty glass of whiskey with a cigarette butt floating in it. A cornet case stood on one end by the bureau, and next to it another cornet case, open, with a cornet lying across it, cup mute in the bell. There were no pictures on the wall, no calendar, nothing.

"What the hell time is it?"

"It must be around four," I said. I wanted in the worst way to get a look at those records. They had to be jazz.

He grunted, like he wasn't used to the idea of it being four. Then he said, "You got any dough?"

"No," I said. "I never have any dough." I wondered if I could get him to play some of those records for me.

"Take a buck off the bureau and get me some coffee and a piece of custard pie. There's a greasy spoon around the corner on Twenty-third Street. Meanwhile I'll see if I can get some blood moving in my head."

The way he talked to me gave me a good feeling. It was like we were the same age and were doing something together. I went around the corner to the greasy spoon, got the pie and coffee, and came back to his room. By now he'd got pants and a shirt on, and was sitting on the bed yawning and putting on his socks. His yellow hair stuck up all around like hay. "Put the stuff on the chair," he said. There was room there now, for he'd taken his clothes off it.

"Do you always eat custard pie for breakfast?"

"Yeah. Sometimes peach pie. But I had a liking for custard pie since I was a kid. This here stuff ain't nothing like my sis used to make, but I can choke it down."

"Did your sis always cook at your house?"

"My old lady died when I was nine. Sis had to take over for her, even though she wasn't but twelve herself." He took a swallow of coffee, picked up the pie with both hands and bit off the point. "You always got to eat the end of a piece of pie first."

"Why? I never heard of that."

"Bad luck if you don't." He took another swallow of coffee and another bite of pie. "That's more like it," he said. "We didn't get off work till eight this morning and then Phil wanted to go eat some Chink food. I didn't get to bed till ten."

"I shouldn't have woke you up so early."

"Naw, it's okay. I got things to do anyway." He took another bite of pie and washed it down with coffee. "What kind of a horn you got there? Lemme see it."

I opened the case, and handed him the cornet. He looked at the engraving on the bell. "Hmmm," he said. "Stratton. That baby's been around awhile. Where'd you get it?"

"From Hull House. I rent it." It made me feel kind of proud to be talking about horns with him.

He worked the valves. "Hand me my mouthpiece."

I didn't dare take the mouthpiece out of his horn myself, for fear I'd break something, so I brought the whole horn over to him. He put his mouthpiece in my Stratton and blew a few notes. It amazed me how easy the notes spilled out, like he hardly put any effort into it at all. "Hmmm," he said again. "You cleaned it out recent?"

It never occurred to me you ought to clean your horn. How come Mr. Sylvester never said anything about it? "Not for a while."

"You got to clean out a horn regular."

"I heard of different ways of cleaning your horn," I said. "What's your way?"

"I never heard of any but one way, soap and warm water. You got a little brush for the crooks?"

"Maybe I can get one." I didn't see how I could unless I stole it.

"Just make sure you wipe the water off good afterwards or it'll leave spots. Although in the case of this horn I don't know as it matters too much." He shook his head. "You oughtta put new corks in the valves to cut down on the leaks. Of course it ain't your horn." He finished off the pie and coffee and sat there licking his fingers to get the last taste of custard. Then he said, "How come you got interested in jazz?"

"From hearing you that time we were fixing the pipes down there in the cellar of that joint. I got so excited by it I could hardly sleep that night."

"Naw," he said, "I ain't that good. You ought to hear those New Orleans guys, like King Oliver out at Lincoln Gardens or Paul Mares with the Rhythm Kings. I ain't nothing compared to them."

"The New Orleans Rhythm Kings? I got one of

their records. Is that who the cornet player is?" It kind of gave me a thrill that he was called Paul, too.

"Yeah. Paul Mares. He's one of those New Orleans guys. They're the best. You can't beat 'em. Which record you got?"

" 'Oriental' and 'Farewell Blues.' I've been trying to copy it off the record."

"Oh yeah?" he said. He handed me my horn. "Go ahead. Play it. Let's hear what you sound like."

I took the horn, feeling as nervous as could be. It was one thing to sit there in Hull House with a cup mute in and bang away. It was another to play it for a real musician. The trouble was that I couldn't really get the feeling into it that Mares got—or Tommy got. That bounce, that sparkly feeling. I could play the notes right, most of them anyway, but not the feeling. But I was determined to try. I blew a couple of scales to warm up, and then I started off. About two bars in I hit a clam. I flashed hot. That made me hit another clam, and I stopped, feeling embarrassed and sore at myself.

"Take it easy," he said. "Don't take it so fast. Just play it nice and easy."

It never occurred to me that I didn't have to play it as fast as the Rhythm Kings did. "You mean play it slower?"

"Take it where it's comfortable for you. You ain't Paul Mares yet."

So I started off a little slower, and by the time I got through the first few bars I knew I could do it if I didn't lose my concentration. So I banged away at it, right on through to the end of the second chorus. I quit playing and looked at him, waggling the valves and feeling mighty nervous.

"I'll be damned," he said softly. "I'll be go to hell." He gave me a look. "How old did you say you was?"

Well, now I was glad as could be that Mr. Sylvester had put me through the mill the way he did. "Thirteen," I said.

"Thirteen? Jesus." He picked up his horn. "Gimme a B-flat." I hit the note and he tuned to it. Then he said, "You're banging the beat right on the head too much. It ain't no march. You don't want to hit the beat right on the head. Listen." He lifted up the cornet and played the first eight bars of "The Stars and Stripes Forever." "Now that's the way Sousa plays it—hits the beats right on the head. To play jazz you got to hit the notes off the beat. Like this."

He started playing it again with the jazz in it. Now the music had that lightness to it, like it was dancing, leaping up and down. There was glory in it.

He stopped. "See what I mean? You got to get over hitting the beat right on the head."

I didn't really get it. I could *hear* the difference all right, it was plain as day to me. But I couldn't hear what he was doing that made the difference. "How do you know where the beat is if you don't play on it?"

"That's what you got a rhythm section for. Tap

your foot, whatever. Listen." He tapped a slow tempo with his foot, and played along. Once again there was the floating feeling to it. He stopped. "See, it's more in between the beats."

"Like syncopation?"

"That's what a lot of them writers say in the magazines, but it ain't. Them writers don't know nothing about it. Who the hell told them they could explain jazz to everybody when most of 'em don't know the difference between a tuning fork and a basketball? It ain't just syncopation. You got to take the beats by surprise—get in there a little quicker than they expect or wait until it's just about too late and then jump in."

I shook my head. "I don't see how you can figure all that out when the notes are flying by you so fast."

He laughed. "Hell, kid, you can't *think* about it. You got to feel it. You got to let it happen of its own accord."

"What if you can't feel it?"

"You will. You stick to it and one day it'll come to you and you won't ever have to think about it again." He opened the spit valve and shook a little water out. "All right, come on, we'll try 'Farewell Blues' once and then I got to go see my girl so she don't get salty with me. You take the lead. Just play it like you did before." He stomped four beats and off we went. Well, I tell you, I never felt anything like that in my life. I played it the way I'd learned it, and he played along with me, circling around me, weaving through my line, up and down and around. I couldn't believe it was me; I couldn't believe it was me playing jazz.

Then we stopped. He stood up. "I gotta go. She's probably already sore at me."

"Can I come back, Tommy?" I wasn't sure if I was supposed to call him by his first name, but I wanted to.

"Sure," he said. "I don't mind."

8 IT CAME OUT the way I figured. Pa never said anything more about taking lessons from Tommy Hurd. I don't know if it was his idea, or Ma's; probably both of them, for different reasons. I figured he just threw Tommy's card away and let the whole thing slip from his mind. I wasn't going to bring it up: if I didn't ask they couldn't say no.

I knew I shouldn't make a nuisance out of myself to Tommy. I figured if I went out once or twice a week—every five or six days, maybe—didn't stay more than an hour or so, and brought him his pie and coffee, he might put up with me for a while. I *had* to learn how to put that floating feeling into the music. So that's what I did—hike myself over there every once in a while.

To be honest, I admired Tommy more than anybody. I admired people before. I admired Ray Grimes on the Cubs, I admired Tom Mix and some of those other cowboys in the movies, who raced their horses through rivers and over gullies to catch the bad guys. But I never admired anybody the way I admired Tommy. It wasn't just because he could play jazz, either; it was the kind of guy he was, too. The only thing that mattered to him was jazz. He hardly thought about anything else. Sure, he had some girlfriend he usually went to see before he went to work, and he liked to shoot pool—he had an uncle who ran a pool hall, and when he was a kid he used to hang around there a lot running errands and sweeping up. But I noticed that when he was showing me something about jazz, he'd forget what time it was, and suddenly have to rush out so his girlfriend wouldn't get salty with him.

You take me. I was used to having a nice home, clean clothes, lampshades with fringes on them, a carpet on the living room floor. Pa said he could afford to have a nice home and was resolved to have it. But Tommy, he didn't care about anything like that. He didn't even notice that there was no shade on the lightbulb hanging from his ceiling, that there weren't any pictures on the walls. It didn't make any difference to him whether there was a lampshade or pictures, because he wasn't there anyway—he was somewheres off in jazz land. To him a place was a nice home if it had a phonograph and some jazz records; if it didn't, it wasn't.

I guess that's one reason why he didn't mind me coming around. He could talk jazz to me as much as he wanted and I sat there and soaked it up. He'd play me records he figured I ought to know about—the Original Dixieland Jazz Band, which got a lot of people started on jazz, Bailey's Lucky Seven, the Original Memphis Five and of course the Rhythm Kings—he had all their records, every one of them. He'd teach me tunes, he'd show different ways of fingering certain phrases. We'd play things together, and he began to give me some idea of what improvising was all about. That was another time when those old piano lessons came in useful, for I knew what he was talking about when he explained how you put a melody against the chords.

A lot of times we just sat around and talked. He told me about the gigs he was on—what they were like and who was on them. He told me about going to the South Side, around State Street and Thirty-fifth where there were a whole lot of jazz clubs. "You got to get over there sometime, kid, and hear for yourself. Get yourself a pair of long pants, they'd probably let you in. The Nest, the DeLuxe Cafe, Dreamland, Lincoln Gardens. Places like that. That's where all those New Orleans guys play."

That brought up a question that had been bothering me for some while, for the Black Belt was on the South Side. "Tommy, why do they call it nigger music?"

"That's to set people against it. A lot of white people, you tell 'em jazz is nigger music, they don't want nothing to do with it."

"Well, is it or isn't it?"

"That's a hard one, kid. I don't rightly know. It started down there in New Orleans, and from what you hear it was the colored guys who came up with the idea. But the first we heard of it up here in Chi was these white bands—the Original Dixieland, Tom Brown's Band from Dixieland and such. The colored guys began to come up a year or two later—Duhé, Keppard, Oliver, this here Bechet they all talk about. Nick LaRocca and them white guys from the Dixieland, they always claimed they started it, but Steve Brown—that's Tom Brown's brother, he's the bass player with the Rhythm Kings, a white guy—Steve says LaRocca's full of it, he stole all his stuff off Ray Lopez. Steve told me in New Orleans they got it off the colored. Out there in these country towns down there the colored had these little bands—Steve thinks it started out there. When you get a chance to hear some of these colored fellas play, you figure that might be right. But I don't know. I wasn't there myself."

"So it is nigger music."

He kind of looked at me sideways. "So what if it is?"

So what if it was? That was kind of hard to answer. "Well, a lot of people figure nig—colored people are kind of low down."

Tommy nodded. "Some of 'em are. Some of 'em ain't. You take Calvin Wilson, he's as good a fella as any white man I ever met."

"The piano player you were jamming with at Herbie's club?"

"Yeah. I'd trust him with my wallet and the keys to my place."

It was a hard one. I'd been raised all my life to think of the colored people as low down, and it wasn't easy to change. But I didn't want to disagree with Tommy, and I resolved I'd do like he did, and say colored instead of nigger. "Okay, is it colored music? Or is it white people's music, too?"

"Well, I reckon it belongs to anybody who's willing to take good care of it," he said. "The Rhythm Kings are white and the Oliver bunch is colored and I don't see as there's much difference between 'em. Both from New Orleans of course." He stopped to think about it. "I don't know, maybe you got to give the edge to Oliver. He does stuff with mutes that beats everything. He's got this number 'Dippermouth Blues,' where he works the plunger so nice you think it was a baby crying for its ma."

"What's a plunger?"

Tommy laughed. "Why you ought to know, of all people, kid. It's the rubber part of a plumber's friend."

That sure surprised me. "What you use for unstopping toilets?"

"That's it. He works it over the bell. It's just

James Lincoln Collier

uncanny." He picked up his cornet, and began to play real soft, at the same time closing and opening the bell with his hand. It *was* uncanny, too, for he could get all kinds of effects with it—laughing, crying, people talking.

He put the cornet down. "Of course I was using my hand. It ain't nothing to what Joe Oliver can do with a plunger. Or a bottle, ashtray, anything."

Naturally I was all fired up to try it, and I resolved I would, the minute I got home, for Pa had two or three plungers laying around. "So in the end you would say the colored guys are best."

"Well, yes and no. You can learn something from those colored guys, all right. They got something to teach you. A lot of guys get out to State Street whenever they can to listen to them. But in the end you got to run it into something of your own. You take Calvin Wilson. He ain't from New Orleans. Memphis. He didn't grow up with jazz like the New Orleans guys. He learned to play the blues on the guitar from hanging around the colored stevedores on the waterfront. When ragtime got big he switched over to piano—taught himself, all the keys, not just D-flat like those blues players. He played in all those colored saloons down there—Memphis, St. Louis, Sedalia, which was a big ragtime town. When jazz come along he came up to Chi and took it up. He's an all-around entertainer, really. Sings, gets up from the piano and dances while he's playing, writes his own songs. I heard him first in one of Dan Jackson's gambling joints. Tough place."

"Who's Dan Jackson?"

"Colored gangster. Politician, gangster, I don't know what you call him. Runs half the Black Belt. Calvin was in with him, and played his clubs. I started sitting in with him. He didn't mind—give him a rest. That's how we got to be buddies. He ain't a real great jazz musician—still got a lot of ragtime in him. So you can't say every colored guy is a natural-born jazz musician. But I learned a lot from Calvin."

"How come he never plays in your band?"

"Are you nuts, kid? You can't put a colored guy in a white band. White guy in a colored band, neither. Oh, a white can sit in with a colored band and nobody'd say nothing about it. But not as a regular part of the band. The cops would close you down if you tried it. And worse if a colored guy went to sit in with a white band. It just wouldn't happen." He shook his head. "But I can sit in with Calvin. Maybe some time you can get your folks to let you out at night, I'll take you out there. Go to Lincoln Gardens and hear King Oliver. Seeing as I don't start till midnight we could go over there for a couple hours first. You got to get hold of long pants, though."

Oh, it took my breath away to think of going out to Lincoln Gardens to hear Oliver, but I knew there wasn't any hope of it, either. Not until I was older and on my own, anyway. "How come they never made any records?"

"I heard they just went down to Richmond, Indiana, to cut some sides for Gennett, but I ain't seen any in the stores yet."

Gennett was the same label the Rhythm Kings made their records for. "Do you think King Oliver's Creole Jazz Band is better than the Rhythm Kings?" I hated to think that, for I'd gotten loyal to the Rhythm Kings.

Tommy thought about it. "Don't know. All them New Orleans fellas are pretty damn good. A couple of years ago this fella Lawrence Duhé had a mighty fine band at the DeLuxe. Freddie Keppard was in that. Keppard was all the rage until Oliver came along. Freddie got to drinking, that was his problem. I ain't against a man taking a drink, but Freddie took it to where he couldn't play right. Then there was this clarinet with Duhé named Bechet who had everybody talking. I didn't hear him myself. He ain't around no more. I don't know what happened to him."

"These are all colored guys?"

"Colored, all from New Orleans. But I'm not saying as you can take it away from the white guys, either. I don't reckon there's any better bass player around than Steve Brown. And Rop—I'd put him up there with the colored clarinets."

For a minute he sat there thinking. "You know, kid, it's kind of mixed up, when you get down to it.

See, a lot of these guys ain't exactly colored. They're Creoles. Frenchmen, they call them down in New Orleans. You and I might take them for colored, but they'll tell you they're different. Pretty light-skinned, some of 'em. Take this here piano player Jelly Roll Morton—he's as light as you or me. Great player. Speaks good, too. Speaks better than me, when you get down to it. When you look at it that way, you might say these here Creoles are the key to it. Keppard, Bechet, Duhé, Jelly Roll—all Creoles. I guess Oliver's part Creole, too, although he don't look it. I mean they call the band the Creole Jazz Band, don't they?"

The whole thing confused me a lot. It was the way Tommy talked about the colored that struck me funny. When somebody I knew mentioned the colored, you could tell just from the way they talked that they took them to be low down. They didn't have to *say* it straight out—it was just there in the way they put things. If you just called them niggers, that'd do it. But there wasn't any of that in the way Tommy talked about them. For one, he never said nigger. He talked about them like they weren't any different from anybody else. They had their own ways, maybe; I guess Tommy would say that. All people had their own ways, when you got down to it—Italians, Irish, Jews, whatever. A lot of times you could tell who somebody was just by the way they talked, or from their clothes. I could see that just by looking around my own neighborhood. The colored had their ways, too. But leaving that aside, from the way Tommy talked about this musician or that musician, it didn't seem to matter very much where they came from. It was how they *played* that mattered. I could see the justice in that. But it was new to me, and I wasn't used to it.

I never paid Tommy anything and he never asked me to. Of course he wasn't giving me real lessons like Mr. Sylvester. You know, sit there playing exercises over and over until I got them right. But I was wasting a lot of Tommy's time, a couple of hours a week. For a long time I was afraid to bring it up. If he decided he wanted to get paid, there was no way for me to get hold of the money. But not paying him made me feel guilty. Pa had drilled it into us that a man paid his own way. I didn't feel good about getting free lessons from Tommy, and finally I brought it up.

He laughed. "How much could you pay me, kid? A half a buck or something?"

I couldn't even pay him that much, but I didn't say so. Instead I said, "Yeah, around that."

"You know how much I make with Herb Aronowitz?"

"No."

"Seventy-five smackers a week. You think your pa makes that kind of dough?"

To tell the truth, I didn't know how much Pa made. A couple of times I asked Ma. All she ever said was, "That's your Pa's business, he'll let us know if he

wants to. We've always had a nice home and we never missed a meal. That's all we need to know."
But I knew that seventy-five bucks a week was big dough, because most working people considered they were doing good if they made twenty-five. "How come he pays so much?"

"They all do. Everybody wants to get out to dance and they need music for it. There ain't enough musicians to go around. Those fellas with Paul Whiteman, some of 'em are drawing a hundred-fifty, two hundred bucks a week. Of course they double two or three instruments and can sight-read anything you put in front of 'em like they practiced it for a week. Some of 'em could go into the Chi Symphony tomorrow, but they won't because they're making too much with Whiteman. But even a fella like me, who can't read so hot, can make good bucks nowadays. Jazz is popular. It's what a lot of people want for dancing."

"Do you think I'll ever make that kind of dough, Tommy?"

"Sure you will, kid. I saw that right from the first time I heard you play. You just got to keep after it."

But it still didn't explain why he was willing to waste so much time on me, so I asked him.

He shrugged. "I don't rightly know, kid. I ain't one for asking myself a lot of questions I can't answer. It don't do to dwell on yourself too much."

"But there must be some reason."

He sat there on the side of the bed, fingering the

valves and thinking. Finally he said, "Well, you're looking at things from the bottom, kid. I look pretty grand to you. But I ain't so high and mighty as you think. I'm just a guy nobody ever heard of banging away in tough dives like the kind Aronowitz runs. I ain't in it with the Rhythm Kings or Oliver or them New York guys like Phil Napoleon and Miff Mole. I never made no records, I never played in any of them fancy cabarets like Lamb's or the College Inn. Only tough dives. I figure I'll get there some day. But I ain't there yet and it's almighty nice for a change to have somebody look up to me. You take King Oliver. Down there at Lincoln Gardens they put on a Midnight Ramble for whites every once in a while. The place is packed, Oliver's got that many fans. I ain't got so many fans I can afford to be casual about it." He grinned. "You're about the only real fan I got, kid."

You can believe that set me up a good deal.

TWO DAYS LATER my report card came through. Miss Hassler didn't hand it out to me with all the rest. Instead she held it back and told me to come see her after school. "Paulie, you didn't turn in but three or four homework assignments all term."

I didn't say anything. I couldn't. Instead I looked at my feet.

"Do you want to get left back?"

"No," I kind of whispered.

"Look at me." I raised my head. "Paulie, you're not stupid. You know that."

"I guess so."

"If you only worked a *little* you could at least pass. Why can't you do that?"

I couldn't tell her the truth—that music kept getting in the way of my homework. For if I told her that she was bound to tell Ma and that'd be the end of my cornet. "Pa says I got a lazy streak."

"What's your pa going to say when you bring home a report card with nothing but F's?"

I didn't say anything. I didn't want to think about it.

"What will he say?"

"I don't guess he'll like it."

"I don't guess he will, either. Now I want your ma to come in to see me. No ifs, ands, or buts." She gave me a long look, which was supposed to tell me something.

Oh, now I was sorry as could be that I hadn't done some homework. Why hadn't I planned a little more? It wouldn't have been *that* much trouble to do a little homework every night. Why couldn't I make myself see there wasn't anything wrong with planning a little? If only I'd squeezed in an hour or so a night. I could have passed—could have passed a few things, anyway. Why hadn't I? But it was too late for that.

I took my time getting home, dawdling along the street, looking in store windows, watching some little kids play hopscotch on the sidewalk. For once I didn't even feel like playing my cornet.

But even with the dawdling, I ended up getting home. I went on up the stairs. Ma was sitting at the kitchen table peeling potatoes. "Where's John?" I figured I'd confess to him first, so as to practice saying "I flunked" a little.

"He went off with Pa to get a load of pipe."

It was best to get it over with while Pa wasn't around. I took a deep breath. "We got our report cards."

Ma raised up her head, but she didn't stop peeling the potato. She knew what was coming. "Oh?"

I took another deep breath. "I flunked everything." I handed her the report card.

She took the card out of the envelope. "So you did," she said. "It was what I expected." She was being very cool, like I got what I deserved, and she wasn't going to help me out of it.

"Miss Hassler wants you to come to school and talk to her."

"I expect she does." She tapped the report card on her cheek. "You know what this means, Paulie."

Why hadn't I made myself think ahead? What a dope I was. I would have liked to give myself a real hard boot in the tail.

"Ma—"

"Paulie, do you think for one minute your pa is going to allow you to go on with your music after this?"

I felt hot and my hands were clenched by my sides. "I don't care. I won't quit."

She didn't say anything. Then she said, "You better go to your room for a while. And if I were you, I wouldn't be playing your cornet when Pa comes in."

She was right about that, anyway. I went into my room feeling good and sore. "You can't stop me," I whispered under my breath. But I knew they could. For a long time I lay on my bed with my hands under my head, staring at the ceiling, feeling sore at them and sorry for myself. After a while I got up, sat down at the table, took out my math book, and tried to do some problems. I couldn't do them. I was too far behind. I lay my face down on the book. It felt smooth and cool, a nice feeling. But inside me, I didn't feel so good. So I sat up, turned the pages back to the last place where I understood it, and began to catch up.

Pa and John came home at five. By that time I'd put in an hour on my math book, which was more homework than I'd done the last two months put together. I'd got up to around December, I figured. At that rate I'd catch up to the class by June, but of course they'd keep on moving ahead of me. And it wasn't just math, it was English, civics, science, and all the rest of it. It was hopeless. Why hadn't I tried just a little?

After a bit Ma stuck her head in the bedroom. "I haven't said anything to Pa yet, Paulie. Come on out and eat your supper." It was New England boiled dinner, which I loved, but I couldn't take much pleasure in it. Pa was feeling pretty cheerful, for he'd won the bid on a good job, and was talking about buying a truck. He'd been talking about getting a truck for a couple of years. All along he'd said he had the dough, but it didn't do to rush into things. Now it looked like the time was ripe—he knew of a fella who had a secondhand Ford for sale cheap. He figured he'd look into it. Ordinarily I'd have been all excited by the idea that we were getting a truck. But right then I didn't feel like part of the family: *they* were getting a truck, not me.

After dinner I washed the dishes and went back to our room. It wasn't that I was eager to do any schoolwork. I just wanted to get away from Pa and Ma. John was already in there, scratching away at his Shakespeare paper. I shut the door. "I flunked everything," I said in a low voice so Pa wouldn't hear.

John stopped scratching. "I figured you were going to. You didn't do anything all term but play your cornet. What did you expect?"

"Couldn't you even say you were sorry about it?"

"Sure I'm sorry. Who likes to see their little brother get left back? But you brought it on yourself."

"Listen, John, you got to help me catch up."

"I don't 'got to' do anything."

"Please."

"All right," John said. "What's the worst?"

"Math. I'm years behind."

"Where's your book? Sit down here and let's see

how bad it is." He helped me for a while, and moved me up to January, but then he had to get back to his Shakespeare paper. I went on by myself for a while, but I was feeling mighty discouraged about the whole thing, and finally I put on my pajamas and went to bed without brushing my teeth.

Something woke me up. The lights were out, and I could hear John breathing in his sleep. Then I heard Ma's voice. She was speaking low, and I couldn't make out her words, but when Pa came in I could hear him clear enough. I figured that was what woke me up—him saying my name pretty loud. Now he said, "I'm going to chuck that damn cornet in the Chicago River."

I wanted to hear Ma's side of it, so I slipped out of bed and crouched down by the door with my ear resting against the keyhole. "You can't do that," Ma said. "The cornet belongs to Hull House. We're just renting it."

"Then it can go back. I've had enough of Paulie. He's got to learn nobody owes him a living. You give in to him too easy. He's got to learn he isn't going no place without a lot of hard work."

"Frank, he's just a baby."

"No he isn't. That's where you got it wrong. He's thirteen. When I was thirteen I was doing a man's work."

"You had to, Frank. You didn't have any choice. You always said you wanted the boys to get their schooling instead of having to work like you did."

"All right, fine. Schooling. I didn't say nothing about playing rotten music instead of doing his homework. Now that's the end of that. I'm taking that damn thing back to Hull House tomorrow. If he even whistles around this house for a month of Sundays I'm going to do something drastic."

There was a silence, and then Ma said, "Frank, this is one time when you got to give me my way. This is the first time in his life Paulie ever got his teeth into anything. It isn't my idea of what I wanted him to do, and—"

"You was the one who said he had an artistic temperament and should take piano."

"Maybe that was a mistake. Maybe I shouldn't have got him started on that. Heaven knows, I wish he'd gotten his teeth into some worthwhile kind of a hobby, like collecting stamps or building ship models, where he'd learn something. But he didn't. Right from the day he went to that parade with John he took to music, and he's stuck with it for almost a year now. He never stuck with anything for more than a week before."

"I sure as hell wish John had kept out of it."

"If it hadn't been that parade it'd have been something else. He was bound to come across music somehow." There was a silence. "It'll kill him if you take this away from him, Frank. I won't be responsible for his actions. You've got to listen to me about this, Frank. I know Paulie. He's taken his music to heart. There's a lot worse things than that. He's finally got his teeth into something. You can't destroy it."

Pa didn't say anything. Then he said, "He's got to pass his schoolwork. I don't care what he's got his teeth into, he can't get left back."

"I promise, Frank. He'll pass. He'll pass if I have to break every bone in his body. But I want him to keep on with his music."

I couldn't listen anymore, for I was all swelled up inside and so confused the only thing I wanted to do was cry. Ma wasn't against me after all. But I couldn't cry, for it would wake up John. He'd want to know what was wrong, and I sure didn't want to talk about it. So I crawled back into bed, pulled the covers over my ears, and by and by I went to sleep.

9 FOR TWO DAYS nobody said anything about it. For one thing, Grampa Horvath got sick again. Ma and Pa were worried about him, and Ma had to keep going out to the North Side to see him.

I was careful to do my practicing over at Hull House, or at Rory's, and didn't touch the horn at all when Pa was home. Besides, I was still trying to get some homework done each night. It was a struggle, especially the math. English and civics were easier because what I was supposed to have learned before didn't matter so much to understanding what we were learning now. I mean I didn't have to have read "Oh Captain, My Captain," to understand *Lamb's Tales from Shakespeare*. But it was a struggle, even so.

Finally one afternoon Ma cornered me when I got

home from Hull House. "I talked to Miss Hassler today," she said. "You should appreciate her, Paulie. She's got your interests at heart."

I figured that was true—at least she thought she had my interests at heart. "What did she say?"

"She said she knew you weren't stupid, and she could see from talking to me that you came from a good home. But you were always daydreaming in class and hadn't done a lick of homework for weeks. So I explained it to her."

"You told her about playing cornet and all?" I wished she hadn't: it was my business, not theirs.

"Of course I did. I didn't want her to think you were a lamebrain. I wanted her to understand why you weren't studying. She said she was glad I told her, for now she could make sense of it. She said you could still pass for the year if you worked at it. She said if you stayed after school she'd help you catch up. But she said you have to show a willingness to work, otherwise she'd just be wasting her time."

But if I stayed after school I wouldn't have much time left to go over to Hull House and practice. "Ma, I—"

She put her hands on my shoulders, crouched down in front of me, and stared into my face. "Paulie, Pa was all set to throw your cornet in the Chicago River."

I didn't say I already knew that. "Ma, he couldn't do that. It belongs to Hull House."

"I told him that. It doesn't matter, Paulie. If you

don't pass, that's the end of music for you. Pa was going to take your cornet back to Hull House."

"I would have run away."

She went on looking me in the face. "No, you wouldn't have, Paulie."

"Yes, I would have."

"No, you wouldn't. You wouldn't do that to me."

I didn't know if I would. I might or I might not. I decided not to say anything.

"Now you listen to me, Paulie. I talked him out of it. I said if he let you keep on with your music, I'd see to it that you passed. I put myself on the line for you, Paulie. I want you to promise me you'll do it."

I looked down at the floor. Even before I got interested in music it was a struggle to get myself to do my homework. "I don't know if I can, Ma."

"Paulie, look at me." I looked up. "You can pass. Miss Hassler said you could, and she's willing to help you. But you have to put in the time, even if it means skipping music practice for a while."

I felt just awful. She'd gone to bat for me, and now I didn't know if I could get myself to study. "I'll try, Ma. I promise I'll try."

She shook her head. "That's not good enough, Paulie. You've got to promise me you'll do what's necessary to pass. You've got to promise me you'll stick with it as long as you have to, to get it right. Otherwise I'm going to take that cornet back to Hull House myself."

How could I promise when I didn't know if I could

make myself do it? But I had to. I took a deep breath. "I promise."

WHAT WITH NOT daring to practice around home in the evening when I was supposed to be doing my homework, I wasn't getting along as fast as before. Still, I was making progress. By this time I'd got beyond copying what Paul Mares played and was trying to improvise something new for myself. I wasn't too good at it. Tommy Hurd had showed me how to work off chord changes, but it was one thing to know the idea of it, and another to sit down and do it. A lot of times nothing would pop into my head and I'd fall back on the melody. Tommy said there was nothing wrong with playing melody, you could make the melody swing, too. But still, I wanted to improvise; wasn't that what jazz was all about?

At night I studied. Or to be honest about it, tried to study. It was an awful struggle. I had to fight myself every step of the way. I'd sit down at the table in our room with my civics book and start memorizing the natural resources: coal and iron ore for this one, timber and rubber for that one. The next thing I knew I'd be leaning back looking at the ceiling, to see if the cracks in the plaster made some kind of picture. Or I'd set out to write a report on the solar system explaining why the planets didn't crash into each other when they went around the sun. And about fifteen minutes later I'd realize I was staring out the window to the apartment across the street where Mrs. Winterhalter was waggling her big rear end while she washed the dishes.

But in the end, by forcing myself hard, I generally managed to get some homework done. At least I'd have something to hand in, so Miss Hassler would know I was making an effort. And I didn't do too bad in my classwork. I was a pretty good guesser, and a lot of time I came up with the right answer to some question. But tests were a problem. The truth was, no matter how much homework I did, nothing seemed to stick beyond a day or two. I'd get something learned, like the natural resources of someplace nobody ever heard of, and the next day I could usually haul up enough of it to answer a couple of questions. But by the end of the week, when we had a test on it, I couldn't even remember the names of the places we had studied, much less their natural resources. I never once got better than a C, and about half the time I flunked—fifty-seven, sixty-three, something like that. It was touch and go. Each night I'd tell myself to grit my teeth and bear down hard; but no matter what I told myself, there I'd be once again staring out at Mrs. Winterhalter's fanny.

Every once in a while Ma'd go to see Miss Hassler. She'd say, "Miss Hassler says you're doing a lot better than last term. She says she can see you're trying. But she says you've got to do a little better."

"I'm trying as hard as I can, Ma."

"You've got to try harder."

Once I asked Tommy how he did in school. "Oh, I got by," he said. "I wasn't no great shakes in English. My people didn't speak too good. But I had a knack for math and science and I got by, until I had to quit."

"Why'd you quit?"

"My old man worked in the stockyards. He got his leg busted by a steer one day. Sis was working in a sweatshop sewing pockets on shirts, but her boyfriend always took half her dough. Of course with Ma dead that left me. I used to deliver newspapers before school—got up at five every morning. After the old man got hurt they took me on full time. Big twelve dollars a week, but it saved us. We ate mostly potatoes and fried fatback all that winter. But Pa's leg didn't heal right, and by the time he got to working again I'd been at it for a year and wasn't of much mind to go back to school."

"How old were you then?"

"Thirteen. I wouldn't have gone beyond fourteen, anyway. By that time I was playing around a little bit. Kids' tea dances, social club picnics. I saw pretty quick I could make a helluva lot more dough playing music than I could delivering papers, and by the time I was fifteen I was in the union."

It was funny: Tommy'd had it mighty hard, what with his ma dying, his pa getting hurt, and eating fried potatoes and fatback all the time. But the truth was, I envied him. When he was my age he was free to do what he wanted. Of course he had to work. But he was already building himself up in the music business, and I was stuck.

"Tommy, how long do you think it'll be before I'm ready to play a dance job?"

"You play good enough already, but you got to know more tunes. You go out there on a dance job, they want to hear all the latest stuff. The kids want the new hot tunes, the old folks want waltzes, somebody always asks for a polka. You got to be ready to play them."

"How am I going to learn them?"

"Get hold of the sheet music. Or learn 'em off records."

"I haven't got enough money for that."

He shrugged. "Go to dances, get around to the clubs. Carry your cornet with you, they'll think you're in the band and let you waltz in."

"Do you think I'd be able to get in to hear Oliver or the Rhythm Kings?"

"I thought your old lady wouldn't let you out that late," he said.

"But if she did."

He thought about it for a minute. "I tell you what, kid, maybe one afternoon we go out to the Stroll and look up Calvin. Calvin's a big man out there. He could get you in anywhere."

"What's the Stroll, Tommy?"

"That's what the colored musicians call the area around Thirty-fifth and State. There's nothing official about it. They stroll around there and catch up on the news—who's working where, if some big name is coming to town."

"I would love to go there sometime."

"We'll do it sometime, kid."

I struggled on through April and May, getting a sixty-five here, a seventy-three there, right on the edge the whole time. June came and that made it even harder, for all the while I sat there in our room trying to get natural resources to stick in my head, I could hear through the open window everybody out on the street in the last daylight having a grand time—kids shouting, grown-ups sitting on the stoops arguing among themselves, cars honking, horses clip-clopping along towing the ice wagon or the fruit and vegetable carts.

Finally the last day came. I could hardly sit still in class. The day wore along, minute by minute. Then there we were, lined up to get our report cards. When Miss Hassler came to me she said, "Paulie, wait a minute, I want to talk to you."

I stepped out of line, my heart beating fast and waited until all the other kids were outside on the street whooping it up. Miss Hassler stood there with one last report card in her hand.

"Did I pass?"

She looked at me for a minute. "No, Paulie. Not really. But I squeezed you through. Your mother's such a nice lady I didn't have the heart to do it to her."

I was saved. But I knew there wasn't any hope I'd be able to put myself through that kind of torture for another whole year. There wasn't a chance of it.

10 THAT SUMMER I got it. It came all in a rush, almost in five minutes. One minute I was trying to figure out what jazz was, and the next minute it was coming out of the bell of my cornet. Why it happened when it did I'll never know. It was one of those times they were using the room at Hull House for a dancing class and I was over at Rory's. Of course Pa wasn't going to let me lay around the house all summer playing the cornet, and took me out on jobs whenever he figured I could make myself useful. But a lot of days he couldn't use me and let me stay home. I was getting in a lot of practice.

By this time Rory had got used to jazz. He'd heard the Rhythm Kings' record of "Farewell Blues" so many times he didn't have any choice but get used to it. I had six or seven records by then. Tommy had given me a couple that were pretty near worn out, and every once in a while at some kid's house I'd come across a good jazz record mixed in with pop stuff like the Aaronson's Commanders or the Benson Orchestra of Chicago, and I'd beg it off him. I had two King Olivers, another Rhythm Kings, the Original Dixieland Jazz Band's "Livery Stable Blues," which made them famous, a Louisiana Five, and a couple more. I had to keep them at Rory's and take a chance on Mrs. Flynn breaking one when she got to drinking beer and crying. She didn't care much for that kind of music anyway, she said. "Danny Boy" by John McCormack was more her speed.

Jazz was getting to be all the rage that summer of 1923. Every time you turned around somebody was raving over a swell new record, a swell new musician, a swell new band. It seemed like every week King Oliver or Jelly Roll Morton or the Rhythm Kings had a new record out. Tommy was talking about a new cornet player named Bix something, who was with a band called the Wolverines. Of course the blues had been hot for a couple of years, and Bessie Smith was getting to be big. I couldn't hear most of these people, because naturally Ma wouldn't let me stay out that late. It made me feel left out of things, like when everybody else is going to a picnic and you can't go because you're sick in bed.

Anyway, jazz was getting to be a big number. Rory wanted to be in on it, so he was game to let me practice over at his house. We'd take the phonograph out on his porch. Rory would practice spitting through the clotheslines down onto the kids in the yard, and I'd play along with records.

I was playing along with Oliver's "Snake Rag," when all of a sudden jazz began to come out of the bell of my cornet. I was so surprised I stopped dead. "Did you hear that, Rory?"

"Hear what?"

"What I was playing." I was all nervous and excited, for I didn't know if I could get the same thing again.

"I guess I wasn't paying attention."

"Well this time listen." I put the needle back to the beginning of the record, picked up the cornet, and plunged in. Here came the jazz again. I could hardly believe it—I couldn't believe that it was me playing the stuff coming out of the horn. I didn't want to ever stop; I wanted to keep on going and going. But of course the record ended, and I put the horn down.

What made the difference? I wasn't even sure I knew—something to do with not hammering down on the beat all the time to make it go, like Tommy said, but letting the beat take care of itself so I could prance around on top of it. Some idea like that. It was hard to explain, but I could see now why they were always saying that you couldn't learn how to play jazz—couldn't just take lessons in it, the way you could learn how to play a march just by following the rules. With jazz, you had to have a certain attitude. You couldn't wrestle it to the ground, you had to let it happen to you. Something like that, anyway.

I put the needle back on the record and played along with it again, trying to figure out exactly what I was doing. I couldn't, and I started to play it a third time, but Rory put a stop to it. He was all for jazz, he said, but there could be too much of a good thing.

I could hardly wait to get down to Tommy's and show him what I could do. Maybe Rory wouldn't know the difference, but Tommy would. The problem was that just then Pa ran into a job he could use me on every day. I think he had a hunch that I wasn't long for school, anyway, and he wanted to start training me for the plumbing business. It wasn't anything you could even argue with him about. He had it all planned out.

On top of it, Ma was leaning on me hard to get a head start on my schoolwork for the next year. Of course, she didn't know that Miss Hassler squeezed me through, but she could see by my grades that it had been mighty close. She went down to the library, got out a speller and a math book, and drilled me whenever she could catch hold of me. Poor Ma, she was going to hate it when I turned out to be a jazz musician living in a room with a bare lightbulb and records scattered on the floor. But maybe after a while I'd do real good at music, have a fancy apartment and ride around in a swell new car. That would be more cheerful for her.

Anyway, Ma didn't catch up to me with the speller

too often, for Grampa wasn't doing any better, and she was over there a lot, tending to him.

Between one thing and another it was a week before I got down to Tommy. In the end I was disappointed. I played for him in my new way, but he wasn't as impressed as I figured he would be. All he said was, "Yeah, sounds good, kid. You been making a lot of progress this summer."

"It was the first time it sounded like jazz to me," I said.

"Oh, I wouldn't of said that." He took a sip of coffee. "Listen, can you get away tomorrow afternoon? I'm subbing for a fella at a tea dance over on Halsted up near you somewhere. If you brought your horn around maybe you could sit in."

He said it so casual, like he could have done it anytime, but it was a shock to me. I'd never actually heard a jazz band live, except that time at the Society Cafe, and here he was asking me to play with one. My mouth fell open. "Do you think they'd let me?"

He shrugged. "You know how it is. Some fellas don't mind about sitting in, some do. There's no harm in asking. I don't know about these here fellas—they got a pretty good opinion of themselves. They call themselves the Austin High Gang, and they like to think jazz is their private secret."

"Who's in it?"

"I don't reckon you know their names. They're mostly around my age—a little bit younger, maybe. Saxophone player named Freeman. Dave Tough on drums. The star's the clarinet—Teschemacher. I don't know any of 'em except to say hello to."

"How come you're subbing?"

He shrugged. "Search me. Freeman got hold of me and said their cornet, McPartland, couldn't make it. It's only a tea dance, but what the hell, it's five bucks."

Well, I was so nervous I could hardly eat supper, hardly go to sleep that night. There were about sixteen things that could go wrong, and one of them was bound to. Pa could decide he wanted me on a job, Ma could decide to drill me on spelling. What about my clothes? I'd have to dress up as good as I could, and if Ma saw me combing my hair, much less cleaning my fingernails without being told, she'd know something was up.

What I did was get up bright and early and take the garbage down. Then I sat under the stoop as long as I dared, hoping Pa would go to work. Finally he did. I went back upstairs. "Where've you been all this time?" Ma said. "Pa was looking for you."

"I took the garbage down. You're always complaining if I don't do it, and now you're complaining when I did it."

"It doesn't take a half an hour to take the garbage down. I suppose you were sitting on the stoop, daydreaming."

I decided she might as well think that. "It wasn't a half an hour," I said.

I spent the morning staying out of sight in our

room, pretending I was studying my speller. Around noon Ma sent me out to fetch some stuff from the store. She fixed fried-egg sandwiches for lunch. I was too excited to eat, but I forced myself, so she wouldn't get suspicious. After lunch I hid out in our room for another hour. Then I took a clean shirt and a necktie out of the bureau and stuffed them into my cornet case. I told Ma I was going over to Hull House to practice, and lit out for Rory's. I told Rory what was up. He was all excited, and wanted to go along, too. I said I didn't know if he could get in or not, and he said it didn't matter, he'd walk me over anyway. So I put on the clean shirt, and then I picked up the tie. The only time I ever wore a tie was to church on Christmas and Easter, and once when Ma took me and John to the photographer to get a picture to send to the relatives. I didn't have much of an idea how to tie one, and Rory had even less of an idea, for Mrs. Flynn wasn't a big one for dressing up, and Rory didn't have a tie.

But he was bound to give advice. "That isn't right, Paulie," he said. "You got to wrap it around the other way."

"If I wrap it around the other way it'll come apart."

"No it won't," he said. "Try it."

I tried it. "See, Rory. I told you it'd come apart."

"You didn't do it right. You got to push it up through there and then around here."

"I could do that easy enough if I had three hands," I said.

"Like this," he said, grabbing on to one end.

"Leggo, you're strangling me." But in the end we got a knot that I figured would pass—about the size and shape of a crabapple, I had to admit, and the thin part of the tie stuck out below the fat part a couple of inches, but at least I had on a necktie. Then we flew out of there and over to Halsted Street.

The tea dance was being held in a Jewish temple and was supposed to run from four o'clock to six. Not being Jewish, I didn't know what the dance was for, but it didn't matter. We marched up to the front door. A fat guy in a yarmulke was standing there. "I'm with the band," I said.

He pointed over his shoulder with his thumb. "Around back," he said. "Musicians around back."

We went down the alley, up a short flight of iron stairs and in. There was a low stage at one end of the room, flowers in vases on tables against the wall, a couple of potted plants. Already a bunch of kids dressed up in suits and dresses were milling around. Tommy and the others were on the stage— saxophone, another saxophone doubling on the clarinet, drums, piano, banjo. Tommy looked at me, but didn't say anything, just went on warming up. Me and Rory went down to the bandstand where there was a row of chairs against the wall, and sat down. I felt pretty nervous. We couldn't get away with claiming we were with the band when we weren't up there playing. I tried to think up a good story, like how a couple of the musicians weren't feeling too good, and we were there just in case. It didn't seem like a very good story; luckily, nobody bothered us.

Then the band started to play and I was in my glory. I sat there tapping my foot, swallowed up in the music. The world around me was gone—Rory was gone, the dancers were gone, the temple was gone—the only thing in the world for me was the music. On and on it went. Time stopped moving.

Finally they took a break. Tommy laid his horn on the piano and came over to me. The other musicians drifted outside into the alley. Tommy put his hand on my shoulder. "You got your horn?"

I gestured down under my feet. "It's there."

"I talked to the fellas. This clarinet player, Tesche-macher, he's the leader. The one with glasses. He said to come up at the end of the next set for a number." He stuck his thumb at Rory. "Who's this? He want to sit in?"

"That's Rory I told you about. He doesn't play anything."

"My ma has a phonograph," Rory said. "Other-wise Paulie wouldn't pay me no attention at all."

"Shut up, Rory," I said.

"I'm going to catch some air," Tommy said and went outside.

I didn't know how I was going to stand waiting

through a whole set. I was nervous and excited as could be. What if I made a mess of it? What if I hit a couple of clams and couldn't get straightened around? Tommy always said you got to allow for clams: the trick was to forget them the minute you hit them. Some musicians, he said, you'd go on hearing a clam for eight bars afterwards. If you hit a clam, forget it and go on.

But suppose I didn't forget it. Suppose I hit a clam and froze up—just stood there with my cornet up to my lips and nothing coming out? Finally I said to myself, damn it, I'm not going to freeze. I'm going to play it just like I was sitting on Rory's back porch. Still, I wished somehow I had a chance to warm up.

The musicians came back, joking quietly about something. Again I fell down inside the music, but this time I listened more careful, so as to get some idea of what I might run up against: the kind of back-up figures they were using, the order of solos, if they gave the bridges on the ensemble to the banjo the way bands sometimes did. Playing a tea dance for a bunch of kids wasn't a big job—two or three hours, five bucks a man, and then they'd go off to their regular jobs, if they had any. With a sub in there on cornet they wouldn't be able to play any little head arrangements they'd memorized. They were just jamming, sticking mostly to pop tunes the kids knew, like "The Japanese Sandman," "Wabash Blues," "My Buddy." Generally Tommy played the lead, but sometimes he'd lay out, the clarinet player would switch to sax, and then two saxes would har-monize on the melody. It was a nice effect. I won-dered if they worked that stuff out in advance, or were faking it. Tommy said a good musician was supposed to be able to cook up a harmony part on the spot.

So on they went, and after they banged their way through "My Honey's Lovin' Arms," I saw Tommy looking over at me. He gave a little wave. My heart jumped. I grabbed my cornet case and trotted up onto the bandstand. "My God, Tommy, the kid's still in knee pants," Teschemacher said.

"It's all right, Tesch. These kids ain't gonna no-tice."

"Okay, kid. What do you want to play?"

"Farewell Blues," I said. I'd played that thing al-most every day for six months. I wouldn't have thought of playing anything else.

"Stand here by me," Tommy said. "Back me up until you get loose. When I point, take your solo."

"Solo?"

"Sure," he said. "What the hell's the point of sit-ting in if you don't get a solo?"

That sure took me by surprise: I didn't have any idea they would let me play a solo, and it scared me some. But I didn't have time to be scared, for Tesche-macher was counting off, and then we were into it. I played along behind Tommy, so quiet at first I could hardly hear myself. Just being up there on the stand with real jazz musicians excited me so much it didn't matter whether anyone could hear me or not.

What surprised me most was the difference it made to play with a real rhythm section. I could feel it going through me in a way I couldn't playing with a record. That was the most exciting part of it— having that rhythm there to float on.

After about sixteen bars I remembered I wasn't up there just to feel good; I was supposed to make music. I began to blow out a little, trying to find something to put in behind Tommy—sometimes just a couple of harmony notes, sometimes a little idea to fill in a gap. We came to the end of the second chorus. Tommy swung around, pointed his cornet at me, and blew a little run-up figure to send me off.

It took me by surprise, but luckily I was already into a little idea I was going to use to bridge across from one chorus to the next. It came out stark naked, and scary: ready or not I was playing a solo. To get a grip on myself I dropped back onto the melody, which I'd played hundreds of times, and stuck with it through the first eight bars. But it wouldn't prove anything to me or anybody else if all I played was melody. I had to take a chance and turn myself loose. So I ran up a scale to a G, and hit a clam—missed the G and got a note that was part E but mostly broken glass. Forget it, I told myself. Forget it. I ran back down again nice and firm to a middle C and I was all right. I sailed on to the end, feeling better and better. By the time I hit the turnaround I was game to take another chorus. But Tommy came back in with the lead, I fell in behind him, and we jammed on out to the end. I stood there, holding the cornet by my side, my hands shaking. I was a jazz musician.

Tommy put his arm over my shoulders. "You did good, kid."

Teschemacher put the cap over his mouthpiece. "Yeah, you were all right, kid. Tommy must have taught you something. You know all the tunes?"

I thought about lying, but Tommy was standing there. "A few," I said.

"Stick with it," Tesch said. Then they all went off the stand and out into the alley.

Rory and I followed them. They stood around talking. I figured that me and Rory would stand around and listen to them talk, just so we could feel like we were jazz musicians, too, but Tommy gave my shoulder another squeeze, and said, "See you around, kid." I guess there was a limit to how much they wanted kids our age around.

11

AFTER THAT, ANYTHING to do with school went flying out the window. Same with the plumbing business. I was a jazz musician, and that was that. What difference did it make that Pa had a good thing set up for me and John? I didn't want to have anything to do with it. John could have it, and the money that went with it, too, even if we could end up on Easy Street the way Pa figured—put on a suit and tie and never pick up a wrench again. What did any of that mean to me? What did I care about a suit and a tie? What did I care about Easy Street? The only thing that meant anything to me was standing up on some bandstand with that rhythm sliding through me, flinging out a string of notes like a shower of water drops shot out into the sunlight.

Sure, maybe I'd get rich and maybe I'd get famous, and maybe I wouldn't get either. It'd be nice to be rich and famous, I figured. But getting rich and famous wasn't the point of it. The point was that rhythm and those notes like drops of water flying in the sunlight. That was all I wanted, ever, and I wasn't going to let anybody get in the way of it.

Why couldn't they give me any credit for how good I was doing with my music? By now I was about the best kid in the Hull House band—even Mr. Sylvester admitted that. He said, "Well, Horvath, you got a ways to go, but it wouldn't surprise me too much if you got there." I told Ma that. All she could say was, "That's fine, Paulie. I'm real proud of you. But you've got to remember, your schoolwork comes first." It hurt me when she said that. It sure didn't make me any more interested in doing homework.

I spent the fall on a roller coaster—up half the time when my playing was going good, down the other half when I got a thirty-five or something on a test, and remembered how hard Ma was going to take it when I got left back.

But I was making my way into jazz. Whenever Tommy had something he figured I could handle he'd bring me onto the gig to sit in for a few numbers. The first two or three times he stayed up on the stand and played along with me. But when he began to see that I could do okay by myself, he took to going outside for a breath of air when I was on the stand, and let me carry the lead for a couple of numbers. I was building up my confidence, and I was learning new tunes, too, for while I was waiting my time to go up and play, I'd memorize a couple of tunes, and work them out on my cornet later on.

Tommy fixed me up with a new mouthpiece, too. The one I'd been using had come with the Hull House horn and was probably as old as the horn. The cup was too shallow, Tommy said. I'd get a fuller sound with a deeper cup, and he gave me one he figured was right for me. He said it was one he'd bought by mistake and didn't like but I didn't believe it; I was positive he'd gone out and bought it for me. And he was right, for I did get a better tone with it.

But I was in trouble at school almost every day. My eighth grade teacher, Mr. Ward, wasn't the type to squeeze anyone through. In fact, he was the other way around. Whenever I didn't do my homework, which was mostly, he took it as a personal insult. By October I could see clear enough that he was going to leave me back if I gave him the least chance. The only way I could pass was to quit everything else and spend my waking hours doing schoolwork. There wasn't any hope I could make myself do that, and I didn't even bother to try.

I guess Ma had an inkling of what was up. She was always asking me how I was doing at school, if I had done my homework, and such. But the fact was that she had a lot of other things on her mind besides me. Grampa had took for the worse. It was nip and tuck if he'd pull through and Ma was always running over there to see to things. He was Pa's father, of course, not hers; but being as Pa's brothers and sisters weren't around, she took the whole thing on herself. That was the way Ma was; and I guess that compared with Grampa dying, whether I did lousy in school or not wasn't so important.

Pa was mighty busy, too. Things had got slack after the war ended in 1918, what with the war industries slowing down and the soldiers coming home and looking for jobs. But by 1923 the papers were full of talk about prosperity: everybody was to have a chicken in the pot and a car in the garage. Pa had more work than he could handle. He had John out on jobs so often, for the first time in his life he missed turning in a couple of homeworks; and me out there, too, whenever he could catch up to me, for I was quick to get out of there on Saturday mornings and hide out at Hull House. Once he even sent John over to Hull House looking for me. Finally Pa bought his truck, a 1919 Ford and took on a couple of extra men, so me and John wouldn't miss too much schoolwork—not that it mattered in my case. Pa came home late pretty frequent, and sat there with a pencil planning the next day's work while he ate his supper. He said, "When you're paying a man a day's wages you better be damn sure you got work for him to do."

But busy as they were, they had an eye on me, too. I tried to keep my mouth shut about music, and do my playing when Pa wasn't around, but it was all I ever thought about and they could see that.

Pa made no bones about it. "I'm giving you fair warning, Paulie. If you don't do good on your next report card, I'm going to chuck that damn cornet in the lake."

Then one day I came out of school and there was Tommy Hurd lounging against a lamppost. "Listen," he said. "I took this damn tea dance for five bucks and now a job on an excursion boat for a double sawbuck come along. Come on down to the tea dance and take over for me. You can have the five. If I cut out after the first set I'll just be able to make it over to the lake on time."

"Five dollars? I can have the whole five dollars?"

"Keep it. You got to start saving for a horn, anyways. You can't go on playing that piece of tin forever."

Well, it was some feeling. It was one thing to sit in here and there; it was another to go out and play my own job. Oh, I didn't expect they'd let me call the tunes and set tempos—somebody else would do that. But I'd be out there on my own. It'd be up to me to set the lead for the others to follow. And I'd get paid. I was making my way into jazz all right. I was going to be part of the whole thing. I walked home smiling.

Naturally I got to the job a half hour before anybody else. Tommy didn't even bother to stay for the whole first set. After about fifteen minutes he called me up, played one number with me and started packing up his horn. "Kid, take it easy. Don't try to hit no home runs." He snapped the case shut. "Call your own tunes and set your own tempos where you'll be comfortable. I gotta run." And he was gone.

Well, that was a surprise: I was just a kid in knee pants and I was going to run the band on the stand. I wondered how the others would take it. I looked around at them, left and right. "Margie," I said, and tapped it off, half wondering if they'd come in behind me. But they did, just like they always did with Tommy—no difference at all. It was amazing to me that they would. But of course they were pros, and would do their job, regardless. And I could see the point of it: I knew what tunes I could play, what tempos I was comfortable at, and they didn't. It made sense to have me call the job. Still, it felt strange, for I wasn't used to it. Maybe one day I would be.

I got through the job okay, and collected my money, a brand new five-dollar bill. I folded it up real careful and stuck it in my shirt pocket. Then I went on home. Pa, Ma, and John were already at the table, eating chicken and dumplings.

"You're late," Pa said. "Where you been? Playing that damn cornet?"

I gave them a big grin and set the cornet case down. "You bet I've been playing that cornet." I pulled the bill out of my pocket. "Look," I said, holding it out where they could see it. "Five dollars. For playing music."

They all stared. It wasn't the Paulie they knew. Then Pa said slowly, "Lemme see that." I handed it over. He looked at it. "Seems like a good bill," he said. He looked up at me. "You sure you didn't steal this, Paulie?"

"Frank," Ma said. "Paulie wouldn't steal."

"I got it playing a tea dance. If you don't believe me, go over to St. Anthony's Parish House and ask them."

"St. Anthony's?" Ma said. "On Halsted?"

Pa sat there staring at the bill and shaking his head. "You really earned this here five dollars playing in a band?"

"Yep. You can ask them."

"Paulie, sit down and eat your supper before it gets cold."

"I'll be goddamned," Pa said.

"Frank!" Ma said.

"Now you can pay me the seventy-five cents you owe me," John said.

But Pa was smart. He dwelled on it overnight and saw what the catch was. The next night at supper he said, "Paulie, I'm real proud of what you did, going out by yourself and earning that five dollars. But you can't let it go to your head. Music isn't no way for a man to make a living. It isn't reliable. Someday you're going to want to have yourself a family, and then you got to have something steady. Now, if you want to go out and play at these here dances and make yourself a little something on the side, why I'm all for it. I like to see a boy who'll hustle for a dollar. But don't think of music as a real job."

"Why isn't it a real job? Look at Paul Whiteman, he makes millions."

"Maybe so, but for every Whiteman there's a hundred out there starving."

I knew there wasn't any use in arguing with him, but I couldn't help myself. He was wrong. "Tommy Hurd does real good. While I was making that five dollars he was out on an excursion boat making a double sawbuck." To be honest, I wasn't quite sure what a double sawbuck was, but it sounded like a lot.

"That the guy who was giving you free lessons? That shows how much he knows about running a business. In this world you don't give nothing away free."

"Will you two stop arguing," Ma said. "Paulie doesn't have to think about his future. He's got his schooling to worry about first." But of course I was so dizzy with jazz there wasn't any room in my brain to worry about school.

My first report card came just before Thanksgiving. Ma and Pa being so busy, they didn't notice I never brought home a report card, and being as John was in high school, he didn't get a midterm report and they weren't reminded of it.

Christmas came and went. By now I was playing little tea dances pretty frequent—maybe every couple of weeks or so. Mostly they came from Tommy, when he had a better job and turned it over to me. But some of the other musicians were getting to know about me, and sometimes they'd send for me. I wasn't anybody's first call, not by a long shot. For one thing, nobody liked having a kid in knee pants on the bandstand. It didn't look good. For another, I didn't know all the tunes. Right about then the big thing was novelty numbers like "Yes, We Have No Bananas," and "It Ain't Gonna Rain No Mo'." I had a little money now, and could buy sheet music to the new tunes when they came along, but I was trying to save for a new cornet and didn't like spending money for sheet music, so I had to scramble to learn tunes the best way I could.

A couple of times I got asked to play dances on Saturday night. Pa was of a mind to let me do it, for I'd earn at least ten bucks and maybe more. Ma wouldn't hear of it. "It's one thing for Paulie to play a tea dance in the afternoon at the temple, or St. Anthony's, where the Father is keeping an eye on things. But I'm not having him out in some rough dance hall where there's liquor and heaven knows what else going on." She was right about the heaven knows what else part: at those low-class dance halls the girls drank beer right along with the boys, and sneaked out in the alley together. I knew about it, because John told me. Ma didn't want him going to such places, either, but he went anyway; he just didn't tell her. Of course, he was sixteen and there wasn't much they could say to him.

12

NEW YEAR'S EVE came and we turned into 1924. By that time I was getting to be enough of a musician so Tommy didn't mind taking me around with him. The other musicians saw that I was his shadow and didn't think anything of it when I turned up with him. One afternoon when I was at his place he said he wanted to go out to the South Side to see Calvin Wilson about something, and I could come along for company if I wanted.

I wanted to go all right—I was game for anything to do with jazz. Besides I was curious. But the idea of going out to the Black Belt worried me. I don't know why it did, exactly. It wasn't likely anyone out there would jump on me. I guess it was just a different world—like going to a foreign country where you didn't know the ropes. But I sure wasn't going to say any of that to Tommy. "Where are we going to meet him?"

"He'll be on the Stroll this time of day."

So we took the streetcar on out there. As we rode along I noticed that there were fewer and fewer white people on the streetcar and more and more colored. By the time we got off, it was almost all colored. The streets were full of colored, too—a few whites mixed in, but mostly colored. I'd never been in the midst of colored people before, and it gave me a funny feeling. There was a strangeness to it: here were all these people dressed in normal clothes, and doing normal things—going into a barbershop to get a haircut, carrying a bag of groceries home, reading a newspaper at the trolley stop. Everything normal, except their skin was black. It felt strange, like looking up at the night sky and seeing orange stars and a purple moon.

But of course I didn't say anything to Tommy about it. He just walked off down the street like he was used to it, passed the rows of stores, taverns, wooden houses, some of them done up pretty nice, some of them shabby. And by and by we saw Calvin Wilson strolling along towards us. He was smoking a big cigar, wearing a derby hat and a black overcoat he let hang open so everyone could see his fancy plaid vest, which matched the lining of the overcoat. We came up to him. "Salutations of the day, Tommy and Little Tommy." He reached into the breast pocket of his suit coat and hauled out a cigar. "Have a seegar, gentlemen?"

"Calvin," Tommy said, "If I smoked one of them things I'd faint dead away." I was curious to try one, but I knew those cigars cost a half a buck apiece, and I was afraid of wasting one.

Calvin held the cigar between his thumb and two fingers and looked at it as if he'd never seen it before. "Why Tommy, this here seegar's mild as mother's milk."

"I bet," Tommy said. "You could put it in a baby's mouth and he'd take to it like candy."

Calvin put the cigar back in his mouth and puffed on it. Then he said, "What brings you gentlemen to the Stroll this fine day?"

"I figured it was time I furthered the kid's education. What's chances of getting him in to hear Oliver?"

Calvin Wilson closed his eyes, and tipped his head back, so that the cigar was pointing up at an angle. He puffed a few times, thinking. Then he untipped his head and took the cigar out of his mouth. "Might as well ask him." He pointed at an angle down the street. "I seen him just now going into that chicken shack over there."

I stared up at Calvin. "You mean I could meet King Oliver? The real King Oliver?"

Calvin smiled. "Couldn't be any realer, I expect. We'll stroll along and see."

My heart was jumping. Would I have a story to tell Rory. Boy, would he envy me. But Calvin was in no rush to get anywhere. He just eased along, greeting everybody as they came along—nodding to this one, shaking hands with that one, stopping to chat with the other. And always polite as could be, asking about everyone's health, how were they feeling, was their ma doing okay, how was business, and such. I could see that he was kind of a star out there. Everybody knew who he was.

But slow as we went, in time we came abreast of the chicken shack just across the street. It wasn't anything but a rundown wooden building with a big window in the front. We crossed the street, and went on in. Tables covered with blue-checked oilcloth, a counter along the back with the stove and icebox behind it, bottles of catsup, blue sugarbowls, salt and pepper shakers on the tables. Being as it was still afternoon, there weren't more than four or five people in the place. And sitting at the far end, with his back to the wall, was a big man in a dark suit, eating. He had a big napkin tied around his neck, and a knife in one hand and fork in the other. Before him on the table was a chicken—a whole chicken—a yellow enameled coffee pot and a bowl—a serving bowl—of mashed potatoes.

Calvin Wilson took the cigar out of his mouth, and strolled along, as easy as ever. "King," he said. "Salutations and joy of the day."

King Oliver looked up from his chicken, and grunted. "How's it going, Calvin?"

I stood looking at him. His face was round, and

there was something wrong with one of his eyes. I wondered if he was blind in it, or if it was just sort of funny. I looked at his lips. He'd been playing jazz for a long time, according to Tommy, and it didn't look like he was having any problems with them—no scars or red marks.

Calvin pointed the cigar back to us. "This here's Tommy Hurd. Cornet player. And that's Little Tommy. Cornet player also. Big fans of yours. When I said you was in here they wouldn't rest until they came to say hello. They own all your records, every last one of 'em." Which wasn't true: even Tommy didn't have them all.

Oliver looked at us for a minute. Then he wiped off his hands on the big napkin hanging down his front, and put out his right. Tommy shook it, and then so did I. It felt kind of funny being proud to shake hands with a colored person, but I was.

Tommy said, "I come into Lincoln Gardens pretty frequent to hear the band."

Oliver looked at him. "Yeah, I thought I seen you somewheres before. You working?"

Tommy shrugged. "It comes and goes, King. Not too bad right now. Herbie Aronowitz has been using me. You know Herb?"

Oliver chuckled. "Yeah, I know Herb. He wanted me to go into one of them dives of his, but the money wasn't worth speaking of. He's a small-timer." He sawed off a chunk of chicken breast.

Calvin looked at the ash on his cigar. "Wants to be

big time," he said. "I heard he was treading on people's toes."

Tommy shrugged. "I don't see anything or hear anything of that. Take my money and go home."

"Herb get himself treaded on one of these days," Oliver said.

He steered the chunk of chicken into his mouth. I wanted to say something, so as not to be left out of the conversation, but I didn't know what to say. Finally I blurted out, "Mr. Oliver, those breaks on 'Snake Rag'—did you write those out, or what?"

"Don't never write anything out. Them fellas are supposed to know what to do."

I wanted to ask more but I decided I better not, so as not to look foolish. Then Calvin looked down at the cigar in his hand and said, "Little Tommy's mighty eager to come into the hall one night to hear the band, King." He went on looking at the cigar.

Oliver dug his fork into the mashed potatoes, "Huummph," he said. He took in a mouthful of potatoes.

Calvin put the cigar back in his mouth and puffed. "I didn't know how it would sit with you, King."

Oliver put down his fork, reached for the coffee pot and filled his cup. "Them knee pants." He put two big spoons of sugar into the coffee. "I don't know about them knee pants."

"I could borrow long pants from my brother," I said. I didn't know as I could, for John was six inches taller than me, but I reckoned I'd figure out something.

Oliver looked at Tommy. "He can play, this here kid?"

"He's gonna be good one of these days."

Oliver picked up his fork and jabbed it back into the chicken.

"Okay, bring him in. But get him out of them knee pants."

Then I noticed by the clock on the wall that it was already after five and I'd have to rush to make it home in time for supper. I wasn't supposed to be late, and there were always questions if I was. But I made it. And as I sat there putting catsup on my baked beans, I could only think of how strange it was to be sitting there, when I'd spent the afternoon in a world Ma and Pa and John didn't know anything about, and wouldn't believe if I told them.

FINALLY THE END of January came and report cards. As soon as I got mine I took a look at it, in hopes that Mr. Ward had taken mercy on me and passed me on something. But he didn't. I shoved the card back in the envelope, put it in my back pocket, and went over to Rory's, feeling rotten. We sat on his back porch, looking out at the clotheslines. "You pass *anything*, Paulie?"

"Nope. What about you?"

"I passed civics and history. Flunked the rest."

"What're you going to do?"

"I'm fourteen. I can get working papers. I guess I'll quit school. Ma's friend Mabel says she can get me a job in the stockroom where she works. It's a good job—indoors, except when you got to make deliveries. What about you?

"I don't know," I said. "I'm scared to go home. When they see this report card that'll be the end of my cornet. Knowing Pa, he won't ever let me touch it again. He's dead set against me being a musician anyway. He's looking for an excuse to stop me, so I can spend the rest of my life in the plumbing business."

"What's so bad about that? I'd take it in a shot. I'd be glad to learn a trade."

"So would I, if it wasn't for that damn music. Sometimes I wish it hadn't got to me the way it did. Sometimes I wish it'd go away and leave me alone."

"Well, then why don't you forget about it for a while? Buckle down to your schoolwork, and come back to music when you get yourself straightened out."

I shook my head, feeling miserable. "I don't know if I can, Rory. I tried it last year. I struggled with it every night for three months and I would have flunked anyway if Miss Hassler hadn't squeezed me through for Ma's sake. There's something wrong with my head, Rory. Hard as I try, I just can't seem to keep my mind on square roots and prepositions. I used to sit there in our room for two or three hours trying to stick stuff like that in my head, but my mind would keep wandering off, no matter what I tried."

"When'll you be fourteen?"

"In a couple of months. But it doesn't matter, for if I drop out of school Pa'll want to make a plumber out of me."

"Most fellas would love to get in on something like that," he said, "Instead of shoveling guts in the stockyards or carrying a hod of bricks up and down a ladder all day long. There's more interest to it."

"John's always telling me that. He's all set to go into business with Pa. He says it's a great opportunity. Business is real good and if it keeps up Pa'll have two or three crews working for him. John says once we get the business built up we'll put on suits every morning and sit around an office all day talking on the telephone instead of threading pipe in some cold cellar." I let out a big sigh. "But I don't care. I got the music hooked into me and can't do anything about it."

"I'm glad I ain't in your fix, Paulie. Ma can hardly wait till I start working and bring in some money. I figure having a job ain't going to be as easy as going to school, especially since I never did much of the work anyway. But it'll be nice to have a little change to jingle in my pocket. I'll have some fun for myself. First thing I'm gonna do after I get a job is find myself a little girlfriend. That's the ticket, Paulie—a nice girl to take out dancing on Saturday night and drink some beer with."

That was the difference between me and Rory— between our families, I guess. We thought different. Pa was always planning something—planning how to build the business up, planning me and John's lives for us, planning for the time when he'd have three crews working for him and could put on a suit in the morning. Same for me. I was planning, too, but it had nothing to do with putting a suit on. Rory and his ma were different: they weren't planners. Pa'd say it might be easier in the short run, but it wouldn't do them any good in the long run. "Rory, sometimes I wished my folks were more like your ma."

He gave me a funny look. "Why?"

"You know—more easygoing. Take things as they come."

"That's pretty funny," Rory said. "I always wished she was more like *your* ma. Nice furniture, carpet on the floor, regular supper every night instead of going down to the delicatessen for fried-egg sandwiches and a bottle of pop. Ma's okay, but if I got myself a little girlfriend, how could I bring her home with Ma sitting around in her old nightie, drinking beer out of the bottle?"

I didn't feel much like laughing right then, but it tickled me, anyway, and I smiled. "I got an idea, Rory. You go on back to my place with this report card and see how you like it. They got a carpet on the floor and you'll get a good supper. But I wouldn't guess what you'll get along with it."

There wasn't any point in stalling it; I might as

well go home and take my medicine. I figured I better tell Ma first. Maybe she could break the news to Pa gently. I said good-bye to Rory and went home, dragging my feet along step by step. Ma was in the kitchen, the ironing board up, pressing Pa's shirts. I stood there looking at her for a minute. Then I took the report card out of my back pocket and held it out to her.

She gave me a steady look. "How bad is it, Paulie?"

"I flunked everything. I knew I would."

She shook her head and went back to pushing the wrinkles out of Pa's shirt with the iron. "I figured it was going to be something like that." She looked up at me again. "You know what it means, don't you?"

I clenched my fists. "Ma, he can't make me quit playing. He can't, he can't. I won't let him."

She went back to ironing. "He can and he will. Poor Paulie. I would have thought you'd try to pass so you could keep on with your music. I don't understand why you didn't. Here was the one thing you knew you had to do, and you didn't bother with it. You have nobody to blame but yourself."

"I tried, Ma, I spent all last spring trying. It didn't do any good."

"Of course it did some good. You didn't get A's, but at least you passed and could go on with your music."

I shook my head. "I didn't pass. Miss Hassler said she squeezed me through because you were such a nice lady."

She looked at me again. "Did she really say that?"

"Yes."

She sighed. "Oh my. We do have a problem here, don't we, Paulie."

"Ma, you got to make him let me keep my cornet."

"Why should I, Paulie, if you didn't even try? If I had seen you were doing your best, and had come close, I might be willing to say something to your Pa. But you hardly did a lick of work all term. At least not when I was around to see it."

I stood there, my fists clenched, feeling wild. "Ma, I didn't try because I knew it wouldn't do any good. I knew no matter what I did there wasn't a chance I'd pass. You got to make him understand, I'm not cut out for school, and a good job and rising up in the world. That isn't me. That's John. I'm not the same as John. I'm not the same as a lot of people."

She shook her head. "Paulie, you're young. You don't have any experience in the world. You have to trust that we know what's best for you."

"Look at Rory Flynn," I said. "He's going to quit school and get working papers. A lot of kids are."

"Paulie, the Flynns aren't like us. That's not a good example."

"You got to beg him, Ma. Don't you see, music is the only thing I ever cared about in my whole life? Don't you see, nothing else matters to me?"

"I see that clear enough, Paulie. That's where the trouble lies. You got to learn there are more important things in life. Your schooling, your family, your future." She lifted the iron so it wouldn't burn Pa's shirt and looked at me. "If only you'd really tried. Oh, I know you'd sit there in front of your book, pretending to study. But you didn't really try."

"I wasn't pretending, Ma. I *was* trying. I just couldn't make myself do it."

She shook her head. "I can't accept that, Paulie. People can always try."

I turned around, ran into our room and slammed the door. Then I flopped down on my bed and lay there with my hands behind my head, staring at the ceiling. Being as it was January the window was closed and it was already pretty dark. The lights were on in the flats across the way, and I could see Mr. Winterhalter sitting in his undershirt at his kitchen table, reading his newspaper, while Mrs. Winterhalter stirred something on the stove. Even with the window closed I could hear the faint sounds of auto horns and the rumbling of traffic. Everybody out there was happy, doing things, going places, and I was stuck.

What was the point in Pa taking away my cornet? I wasn't going to pass, no matter what. He'd put me in the plumbing business, and soon enough I'd run off and go into the music business anyway. Why not let me do it now? But I knew he wouldn't.

I was still lying there like that when I heard him and John come into the apartment. They were laughing about something. I sat up on the bed to listen. Then I jumped up, opened up my cornet case, took out the mouthpiece that Tommy gave me, slipped it into my pocket, closed the case, and lay back down on the bed again. Two minutes later the door opened and Pa came in. "All right, son, give it to me."

I looked at him, but I went on lying on the bed with my hands behind my head. "It's over there. If you want it, go get it yourself."

For a long moment he went on staring at me. Then he said, "Paulie, pick it up and bring it to me."

"No," I said. "If you want it, get it yourself."

"Paulie, I'm warning you."

"I'm not going to get it."

He moved so fast I hardly saw him coming. The next thing I knew he hauled me off the bed and stood me upright. He smacked me across the face with his palm about as hard as he could. Then I found myself sitting on the edge of the bed, blood running out of my nose, across my mouth and onto my shirt. I put my hands over my face and started to cry. I didn't want them to hear, and I tried to hold my mouth shut with my hands. But the sobs kept busting out anyway. After a while I lay down on the bed with my face in the pillow to cut down on the sound. I was smearing blood from my nose on the pillow, but I didn't care. I didn't care about them, or having a decent home, a job, or a future. I didn't belong there anymore.

13

AFTER A WHILE I quit crying, got off the bed and had a look at myself in the mirror. There was blood all around my mouth and my nose was swollen. I wondered if it was broke. Could you play the cornet with a broken nose? I took a look across the room. My cornet case was gone. I took out my handkerchief and cleaned myself up as best I could. Then I went back and laid on the bed in the dark.

They left me alone. John did his homework on the kitchen table, where we ate, and they kept their voices down, in case I was asleep. But I wasn't asleep; I was lying there in the dark, thinking. It didn't seem like I had any choice. I had to run away.

It scared me to think about it. Had I ever been away from Ma and Pa? I thought back. I'd never been away from the family, not for a single night. Once in a while Ma or Pa might go off to visit some relative, but never both at once, unless they took me and John, like a couple of times we went downstate to see our uncle. Actually, it was kind of nice when Ma was away for the night, for Pa would take me and John out to a greasy spoon for supper, and let us choose whatever we wanted—hot pastrami sandwich, hot dogs, chocolate cake, anything.

One way or another I'd always been with my family. It was mighty scary to think of living somewhere without them. I reached in my pocket and felt my mouthpiece, for the comfort of it. Could I take it? Would I get homesick and come crawling home with my tail between my legs? That would be terrible. If I was scared, I'd just be scared. I'd have to stick it out.

I got off the bed, went softly to our bureau, opened my drawer and hauled out the money I had hidden under my shirts. I took it over to the window where some light was coming in, and counted it. Forty-seven dollars. That was a lot of money. But it wouldn't last forever. I'd have to lay out something for a cornet. I probably could get one for fifteen bucks in a pawnshop if I took it without a case. That'd leave me just over thirty bucks. If I was careful I could stretch that out for two, maybe even three weeks. Time enough to get some kind of a job. You could always get a job as a newsboy, although it hardly paid enough to live on. But I wouldn't need much, a place to lay my head somewhere at night and my meals. I could eat pretty cheap—doughnut and coffee for breakfast, cheese sandwich and soda pop for lunch, a plate of beans or hash and a couple of pieces of bread for dinner—maybe a dollar a day for food.

Meanwhile, I'd get some playing jobs going. I'd be able to take jobs at night, now. That'd make a big difference. And without anything else to worry about I could get in four hours a day practice, easy. Go around with Tommy to where his band was playing and learn the new tunes. Sit in where I could. Why not? It was how Tommy got started in music.

The big question was whether I had the guts to do it. I wasn't sure I did. There was only one way to find out. I put the money back under my shirts and lay down on my bed to think about how scary it would be to run away. I can tell you, just thinking about it made me pretty nervous.

After a while the door opened a crack, and there was Ma in the ray of light coming in from the living room. She peered in at me for a minute to see if I was awake. When she saw I was, she opened the door all the way and came in. "I brought you something to eat, Paulie." She put a glass of milk and a plate with a sandwich on it on the table.

"You don't have to feel sorry for me," I said.

She could see me in the light from the door, but her back was to the light and I couldn't see her. "Poor Paulie," she said.

"Don't call me that," I said.

She didn't say anything. Then she said, "There's no use in taking that attitude, Paulie. You brought it on yourself." She turned and walked to the door. Then she turned back. "Eat something. You'll feel better."

I didn't say anything. I waited until she closed the door before I started gobbling down the sandwich and the milk. Then I put on my pajamas, went to bed, and fell asleep right away.

We had two days off because it was the end of the term. I don't know when Pa took my cornet back to Hull House, but it must have been right away, for the first chance I got I took a look in Ma and Pa's room and didn't see it anywhere. He never said anything about it to me. I figured he told Mr. Sylvester the truth—I had to quit music until I got my grades up. I don't guess it was the first time Mr. Sylvester heard that.

Pa let me sit home for a day with an ice pack on my nose to get the swelling down, but the next day he took me off with him and John on a job. I had to earn my keep around there, he said, and if I wasn't going to do my schoolwork, I could start learning the business. It didn't matter to me. So far as I was concerned I was finished with school, finished with the plumbing business. It was only a matter of time. I didn't have much to say to Pa, either—just did what he told me and kept my mouth shut. Once he told me it was no use to sulk, I'd made my bed and had to lie in it. I didn't answer but went on with what I was doing.

I reckoned I'd better wait to run away until school started up again for the second term. That way I could take off in the morning, and they wouldn't miss me until suppertime. I had to figure a way to get some clothes out of the house. Clothes were mighty expensive, and I wouldn't have any money to spare for them. I just hoped I wouldn't grow too much over the next while. Especially my feet: shoes cost a fortune, Ma always said.

On Monday, when school started up again, I went over to Rory's. It was too cold to sit outside, so we sat in his kitchen looking at the calendar for July 1921, which had a picture of the Great Chicago Fire on it. "I made up my mind," I said. "I'm going to run away."

"Oh yeah?" Rory said. "You better wait till your nose unswells. People will think you got some disease."

"It's going down. I don't want to wait too long because I'll lose my lip."

"Are you scared?"

"Yeah, a little."

"Well, you can always go back home."

"No. No I can't. Pa isn't going to let me play no matter what. Sooner or later he'd put me in the plumbing business working ten hours a day every day but Sunday. How would I ever practice? How would I keep my lip up, how would I learn new tunes? I couldn't play tea dances because I'd be down in some freezing-cold cellar threading pipe. I have to run off sooner or later. It might as well be now."

"Maybe there's other things besides music, Paulie," Rory said.

"No," I said. "There isn't. Not for me, there isn't."

"It might be better if you waited till you was older.
Sixteen, seventeen," Rory said. "They couldn't say
much about it if you was seventeen."

"No," I said. "You have to practice every day to
keep your lip. I can't take the chance."

"What's your ma going to say?"

I didn't like thinking about it. She'd backed me up
when Pa wanted me to quit the first time, and here I
was, running away on her. "I can't help it," I said. "If
only she could see I wasn't cut out for school, or
threading pipes, or a nice home. What do I care
about having a nice home?"

Rory shook his head. "I wouldn't have minded,"
he said. "Well, if you need a place to sleep, you can
come here. I got a couple of extra blankets. You can
sleep in the easy chair."

"Yeah, thanks. But this is the first place they'll
look. They're bound to come over and ask you if you
saw me."

"Where are you going? Tommy's?"

"I guess so. To start with anyway. Maybe his landlady has a room to rent."

Monday turned over into Tuesday and Tuesday
into Wednesday, and there I was, still living at home,
still going to school. I couldn't go on like that. Either I
had to give up on running away and quit music, or

leave. But I was having trouble working up the guts to do it. It was scary, all right.

Wednesday night when Ma said she was going over to see Grampa on Thursday morning, I knew my chance had come. Well, that was it—no choice anymore. Either I did it this time or I could forget about it. So on Thursday morning, instead of going off to school, I rambled around the block and then slipped down the alley across the street from our building. There was a row of garbage cans here, and a heap of old boards and bricks nobody got around to cleaning up. I squatted down behind the garbage cans where I could see our front stoop. It was pretty uncomfortable, and after a while my legs began to cramp up. I shifted around to kneel, which eased the cramping, but then my knees began to get sore from the dirt and stones. Running away was more of a pain than I figured on. I crouched up again to give my knees a break. Then I saw Ma come down the stoop, carrying a bag of stuff for Grampa.

Suddenly it hit me that I might never see her again. That was a shock. I went kind of numb, and grabbed on to the rim of a garbage can. In a minute she reached the bottom step, turned off to the left, and walked out of sight. Would I ever see her again? Well, sure I would. It was crazy to think that I wouldn't. But it might be a long time—years, maybe. Suppose she died in the meantime? I shook my head to get that idea out of it. Then I got up, went down the alley and peered out. Ma was out of sight. I crossed the street and went on up to the apartment. Being there alone felt kind of funny. It never happened very much—once in a while, but not often.

But now it was empty, and quiet—no sound of John talking, no sound of Pa's footsteps going into the bathroom, no sound of Ma clanking pots and pans on the stove. I went into the kitchen and sat down at the old wooden table. How many times had I sat there before? Hundreds, I figured; thousands, maybe. I tried to multiply it out, but my heart wasn't in it. When would I sit there again? I looked around. It was all so familiar and homey. Everything in it reminded me of Ma—the big spoons she used to stir soup and beans with, hanging over the stove; the little china teapot she made her cup of tea in every afternoon; the little salt and pepper shakers shaped like swans me and John gave her for Christmas one year when we were little. There wasn't a thing in that kitchen she hadn't touched a thousand times. The kitchen didn't just remind me of Ma; it *was* Ma.

I realized I better get out of there before I busted into tears. I got a paper bag out from under the sink where Ma kept them, and went into our room, trying to keep my eyes from roaming over familiar things. I opened my bureau drawer, shoved my money in my back pocket, loaded some socks, underwear and extra shirts into the bag. I got a pair of pants out of the closet, and my old sneakers, and shoved them into the bag, too. That pretty much filled it up. Then I crouched down and got my cornet mouthpiece out from behind the bureau where I had hid it.

I was pretty nervous, and now I just wanted to get out of there. I had a quick look around to see if there was anything else I ought to take. My history book was lying on my desk. For a minute I thought about taking it down with me and chucking it into the garbage can on my way out. I decided not to. It wasn't mine—I had no right to throw it away. Then I left.

Tommy would be asleep. I couldn't wake him up for a while, but I went out to his neighborhood anyway, killed some time over a cup of coffee, killed some more time in a train station reading a newspaper I found on a bench there. When it got to be four o'clock I bought him his usual coffee and pie and went on up.

He sat up in bed when I came in, rubbing his eyes. "Boy, what a head I got. They brought this guy Bix Beiderbecke into the joint last night, after he got off his own gig. He sat in all night. I can see why everybody's just nuts about him, but boy does he drink."

"Who does he sound like?"

Tommy shook his head. "Sounds like himself. Got a beautiful sound, great ideas. He don't slur so much the way the colored guys do. Pings off the notes like bells. It's a whole different idea from Oliver. I wish I could play like that. He got me to thinking maybe I ought to change my whole style."

"He's better than King Oliver?"

"I wouldn't say that. Different, is all. I got to hear him some more."

"Where was this gig? One of Herbie's?"

"No. Some other crook named Silva."

"Is it regular?"

"So far." He swung his feet out of bed and reached for the coffee. "I need that," he said. "It's just another after-hours dump out in the old Levee." He took another swallow of coffee and blinked his eyes. "I ought to learn my lesson. Some fellas can drink and play. I can't. Lose control of the horn. I was hitting clams all over the place. I wanted to play good in front of Bix and I made a hash of it. These people he came in with, they were loaded with dough and were buying everybody in the band drinks. You don't like to say no to them. I should of ordered gin and told the waiter to fill the glass with water."

"Maybe Bix will come back again and you'll have another chance."

"He said he would. He don't know how long he'll be in Chi, but he said he'd come back." He swallowed some coffee and bit off the end of the pie. "Where's your horn?"

"I don't have it anymore."

"What the hell do you mean, kid?"

"Pa took it back to Hull House. I flunked everything at school and he took my horn back."

"Jesus. That's too bad, kid. Just when you was coming along real good. What can you do about it?"

"I already did it. I ran away." I held out the paper

bag so he could see into it. "I took my clothes and my mouthpiece and left. I got enough money to last me for a couple of weeks. I got to buy a new horn."

"Ran away, did you?" He took another bite of pie and a swallow of coffee. "You sure that was the right thing to do?"

"If I figured I had a chance to pass I would have stuck it out. Give up playing for a little while until I pulled my grades up. But I didn't see where that was going to happen."

Tommy shook his head. "I never did understand that about you, kid. You ain't stupid. How come you can't pass?"

I frowned and looked down at the floor. "I guess I don't want to," I said.

"That don't make any sense at all."

"I know," I said. "That's the way I am, is all." I wanted to get off this topic. "Anyway, it was either run away or quit playing. I didn't see where I had a choice."

"Your ma agreed to your pa turning your horn in?"

"She said I had my chance. She said I should have tried more."

Tommy shook his head. "It's a tough one, kid. I can see that. Now you take me, kid, my family was pretty low-class. Nobody cared much about school. My pa could read and write and do sums enough to make sure his money came out right at the end of the week, but he didn't have much more schooling than that. He didn't care about it very much. I don't know what Ma would of said about it, but she was dead. Sis quit school and went to work as soon as she could, and when Pa busted his leg in the stockyard I had to go to work and nobody ever said anything about it. But you come from a good family. Maybe you ought to think about it."

"I thought about it already. If I go back home I'm bound to flunk again. Pa'll put me in the plumbing business and that'll be the end of music. I don't care about anything else, I'm going to be a musician. They can't stop me."

"Well I can understand that, kid. I was the same way myself—nothing going to stop me from music. But I didn't have nothing else going for me. Without music I'd be working in the stockyards, lumberyards, steel mill, maybe." He ate some more pie and swallowed some coffee. "But you got a chance to get yourself a trade. Something to fall back on if times get hard again. I wish I had a trade."

"I made up my mind," I said.

He finished off the pie, and licked his fingers. "Well if you made up your mind, I guess that's it. I ain't doing such a hot job running my own life."

I didn't get that. It seemed to me he was doing perfect.

"You're doing what you want to do, aren't you?"

He drank the last of the coffee. "Yeah, but what's the future in it? I can't even think about getting married, much less having kids."

"Why not?"

"No decent woman would have me. They say, Tommy, you're a swell musician and we have a lot of fun. But what kind of a husband would you make, spending all your time in dives and coming home just in time to see the kids go off to school? A decent woman, she wants her husband around in the evenings."

"Maybe you could marry some woman in show business. A singer or something."

"That'd be a swell way to raise kids, wouldn't it." He picked a shirt off the chair where he'd flung it when he'd come home. "I guess you can sleep on the floor here for a while. Maybe I can swindle a couple of sheets off the landlady."

"They're bound to look for me here."

"Do they know where I live?" he said.

"No. Not now. But sooner or later Pa'll think of checking with the union and they'll find out."

He finished dressing. "Well, okay. We'll think of something. In the meantime let's see if we can't find some kind of horn in a pawnshop. It can't be no worse than that piece of tin you been playing."

14

WE TRAIPSED THROUGH a half a dozen pawnshops, trying out horns. Finally we came across a nice Selmer which Tommy figured wasn't more than five or ten years old. There were only a couple of dents in the bell, and most of the lacquer was still on. Of course Tommy told the guy it was in lousy shape, needed a lot of work, and got him down to fifteen dollars. Then the guy said he'd throw in a case for another five. Tommy worked him down to three, and I walked out of there with my first decent horn for eighteen bucks. It cheered me up a good deal just to carry the thing back to Tommy's. It didn't matter that the case was worn at the corners and the horn had a couple of dents in it: it was a real horn and it made me feel proud to own it. When we got back to Tommy's place we took the horn apart, and cleaned it out good with warm soapy water and Tommy's little brush. Right from the beginning I got a fuller sound.

Tommy's job didn't start until midnight. We had a lot of time to kill. Tommy decided we might as well go out to the South Side and see what was what. We could get something to eat out there cheap: there were Chinese places where you could stuff yourself with rice and chop suey for a quarter. Maybe we could turn up Calvin Wilson and go around to hear Oliver at Lincoln Gardens.

Well, the whole thing was pretty exciting. I was moving into a brand-new life. No more natural resources, no more pipe wrenches, just plenty of music and excitement. I could hardly believe how much freedom there was in it. I could eat when I wanted to, go to bed when I wanted to, practice when I wanted to, go here or there when I wanted to. Of course I'd have to get some kind of a job, which would cut down on the freedom a good deal. But the rest of the time would be my own. Imagine it—I could go out to hear a great jazz band any time I wanted to, if I had the money.

But still, underneath the excitement, I was homesick and scared, too. I missed the family something awful—my gut kind of ached for them all the time. But I was determined to stick it out, and I resolved not to think about the family or any of that, and concentrate on the good stuff—concentrate on the idea that I was going to be a musician, and nobody could stop me.

We took a streetcar out to the South Side and got off at Thirty-fifth and State. "Here you are," Tommy said. "Smack dab in the middle of the jazz world. There's the Nest over there. Usually a good band there, but it ain't cheap to go in. There's the Dreamland Cafe. A lot of the New Orleans guys played there. This clarinet player Bechet used to play there when it was the Dreamland Ballroom. Down there is the DeLuxe. Everybody played there one time or another—Oliver, Jelly Roll, Bechet, Freddie Keppard—a whole bunch of them."

"What about Lincoln Gardens?"

"That's down on Thirty-first Street."

"Can we go hear King Oliver? He said it was okay."

Tommy stood there thinking about it. "I wished you had long pants," he said finally. "I don't know what they'll say."

"Why would they say anything?"

He shrugged. "Some of these places, like the Dreamland, are black and tans, where whites and colored mix. But Lincoln Gardens is for colored, and they don't always like it for whites to come prying around. If they know you're a musician, and are coming in because you admire Oliver and the rest of the band, that's another thing. You don't look much like a musician in them knee pants." He thought for another minute. "Let's go along the Stroll and see if we can turn up Calvin."

We walked along. The last time I'd been out there it was afternoon, and everything had looked pretty ordinary. Now it was pushing eight o'clock and it was all different—the streets crowded; red, yellow, green, blue lights shining; and music coming out of doors and windows everywhere. And sure enough, in about fifteen minutes we came across Calvin Wilson, strolling along in his derby and a midnight blue overcoat, with the cigar in the middle of his face.

When he saw us, he stopped and tipped his chin up, so the cigar pointed towards the roofs across the street. "Tommy. And Little Tommy. Joy of the evening to you." He shook hands with us both like he was the King of England and we were his dukes. "To what do we owe this honor?"

"We just came out to see how the swells was doing." It was a joke, but there was truth in it, too. Calvin Wilson made a pile of dough and spent hundreds of dollars on handmade suits and handmade shoes, whereas Tommy went around in a brown overcoat with threadbare cuffs and one button missing.

"Ah, but Tommy, you could buy tailor-made suits if you wanted. You don't entertain the folks enough. All you want to do is play the jazz-a-ma-tazz. You got to sing 'em a few songs, tell a few jokes, get in the light touch."

"Well, Calvin, that's your style. It don't suit me."

Calvin blew a bit of ash off the cigar. "Art don't put the bread on the table, Tommy."

"Calvin, how many times have we been through it?" Tommy said. "It don't have nothing to do with art. I couldn't get up and tell jokes if my life depended on it."

"You could learn, Tommy. You can learn anything if the money's right. Nothing wrong with giving the folks a little entertainment for their money."

Tommy shook his head. "What the hell would be the point of it? All I want to do is play the horn. You can keep the money."

Calvin blew on the cigar again. "You young yet, Tommy. You change."

"Maybe. Anyway, the kid wants to hear Oliver. I said I didn't know about it."

"Hummmmm," Calvin said around the cigar. "Them knee britches don't exactly recommend themselves." He took the cigar out of his mouth and blew on the coal.

"Maybe if you was to put in a word," Tommy said.

He blew on the coal again. "Don't he have any long pants?"

"He's getting some," Tommy said. "They ain't ready yet. He's all fired up to hear the band and couldn't wait till they was ready."

Calvin stuck the cigar back into his mouth. "Push 'em down as far as they go. We see."

I pulled the cuffs down, and then I loosened my belt, so my pants hung on my hips. My cuffs were down below my calves. Nobody who took a close look would be fooled into thinking they were long pants, but maybe they wouldn't take a close look. In the end, it didn't matter. The guy at the door gave Calvin a big hello the minute he saw him, and hardly paid me and Tommy any attention at all. And in we marched.

There were tables around the wall, and a big cleared space in the middle for dancing. The place was jam-packed. Overhead was stretched chicken wire, with paper leaves tied to it for decoration. A huge lamp revolved round and round, twirling spots of light across the dancers, but the cigarette smoke was thick as fog, so you couldn't see very much, anyway.

The bandstand was down at the other end of the room. We started for it through the crowd, and right away I noticed that people kept looking at us. We were the only whites in the place. It made me pretty uncomfortable, all those staring eyes. Did they hate having white people come into their place? Or were they just curious about who we were? Maybe we shouldn't have come. Were they sore that we could come into their place, but they couldn't come into ours? I mean they'd never let any colored people into a white club, except to work there—waiters, cooks, musicians, singers. How did they feel about that? I'd talked to colored people before. The building next to ours had a colored porter who followed the Cubs, and I used to go into his furnace room and talk about the ball games with him. The iceman's helper was colored, too. Sometimes on a hot day Ma would give him a glass of water and he'd stand around and talk for a few minutes while he drank it. He'd tell us about buildings six stories high, where he'd carry up two hundred pounds of ice at a time. Then there were the colored women who worked at the laundry down the street. In summer they popped out onto the street for a breath of air every chance they got, and you'd hear them laughing and hollering to each other when you went by.

So it wasn't that I never had anything to do with colored people before. It was just that I never had any kind of a serious talk with one, like did it make them sore that white people could go into their places and they couldn't come into ours? Did they act different when there weren't any white people around? Were they different from whites, or the same—did they have their favorite kind of food like I did, daydream about being rich, want to kiss a pretty girl like I did?

But I didn't get a chance to think about it anymore, for we had got down to the bandstand. There they were, King Oliver and the Creole Jazz Band—clarinet, trombone, piano, drums, string bass, and a second cornet player. The piano player was a woman, which didn't surprise me, for it was popular to have women piano players in bands. I shivered, and rubbed my hands together.

The band had just come in from a break, and was settling down in their seats, shaking water out of spit valves, playing little runs to warm up. Then without any warning Oliver stomped his foot twice on the floor and off they went.

Well it beat the records all hollow. It was just the greatest thing I ever heard. You couldn't describe it, the way they made it rock back and forth. On the records the parts kind of ran together a lot; but in person, each part stood out separate, so you could hear them dart around each other like—I don't know what— like flames in a fire. "What's this number, Tommy?"

" 'Froggie Moore.' Jelly Roll wrote it. Don't you have the record?"

"No."

"Better get it. You got a surprise in store."

The band came to the turnaround at the end of a chorus and then suddenly the second cornet stood up—a short, fat young guy. Next to Oliver, who was big all around, he didn't look like much. But then he started to play. Suddenly the music was different. I couldn't figure out how this little guy was doing it, but he had a kind of leap and spring to his music that no jazz player I ever heard had. I stood there with my mouth open, and that chill running up my spine and crossing my scalp. I didn't say a word until he finished, and then I said, "My God, who is that guy? He's better than Oliver."

"I told you you was in for a surprise."

"But what's his name?"

"Louie, they call him. Or Dippermouth. I never heard anybody call his last name."

"Isn't he something."

"I told you, didn't I?" Tommy said.

"What's he doing that makes it different?"

"There's guys all over Chi trying to figure that one out," Tommy said.

But Louie didn't play another solo and at the end of the set we had to leave so that Tommy could get something to eat before he went on his job.

| | |

TOMMY'S JOB WAS at a club called the Charleston. It was an ordinary cellar joint, like a lot of after-hours clubs. You went down a short flight of cement steps and knocked on a wooden door with a peephole in the center to get in. A dozen tables covered with dirty blue tablecloths were scattered around, with a small space left in the middle for dancing. That was it—no bar, you ordered your drinks from a waiter, who brought them out from a kitchen behind the main room. That way, if the cops came in, they could get the liquor out the back fast.

By the time we got there a few people were sitting at the tables, and the piano player was banging away at "Ain't We Got Fun," to keep them happy. Tommy sat me down at a table near the bandstand, and in about ten minutes I found out another thing about my new life: I could hardly keep my eyes open. I was used to going to bed by nine, ten at the latest. Now it was after midnight and I'd had a hard day on top of it. When they finished the number Tommy told me they'd all get fired if a cop came in and noticed a kid in knee pants snoozing by the bandstand. He told me there was a cot in the furnace room next to the kitchen where the porter used to sleep before he disappeared. Tommy said, "Maybe I ought to ask Silva about the porter's job."

I went on back there. It wasn't very homey, for there was a coal bin full of coal to one side. But because of the furnace it was warm enough. Somebody had left an old brown army blanket on the cot. I curled up inside of it and went to sleep.

When I woke up, a patch of sun was sliding in through a small window high up on the brick back wall of the room, and falling onto the floor in front of the furnace. I sat up on the cot, blinking. Now the excitement was gone—no hot jazz bands, no dance halls and after-hours joints. I was all alone on a cot in a dirty furnace room wrapped up in an army blanket full of stains.

Back a few days before, when I was thinking about running away, I figured I'd be homesick. It was one thing to think about it, another thing to feel it. Being as I was hardly away from my family ever since I was born, I didn't have too much experience with being homesick. It felt a whole lot worse than I'd figured on—made me ache inside something awful. Made me want to light out of there and run back home.

But I wasn't going to do it. It'd make me feel all hollow inside if I gave up music. Besides, I didn't want to give them the satisfaction. They wouldn't say anything. They wouldn't say that they hoped I learned that being a musician wasn't anywhere near as wonderful as I thought. They'd know better than to say anything. But the words would hang in the air all around them, which would be even worse, because if they didn't say anything, I couldn't argue with it. No matter how rotten I felt, I wasn't going to give them the satisfaction.

I put my shoes on and stood up. Maybe if I had a cup of coffee and a doughnut I'd feel better. Or a piece of custard pie.

Then I heard a lock click out in the club and in a minute the furnace room door swung open. The fella standing there was about thirty-five, short and pudgy, hair slicked back, wearing a camel's hair overcoat, and holding a tan fedora in one hand. I figured he was the owner, Angelo Silva.

He looked at me. "Who the hell are you?"

"They said you needed a porter."

He scowled at me. "Who told you that?"

"Tommy." I wondered if I was getting him in trouble for some reason. "The cornet player. I saw him over at one of Herbie Aronowitz's joints and he said you needed a porter."

"How'd you get in?"

"I spent the night here. I didn't have anywhere else to sleep. My old man got drunk and slugged me.

That's the last time he's going to do that. I'm not going back there anymore."

He looked me over. "How old did you say you was?"

"Fifteen?"

"You're sure? You don't look no fifteen."

"I'm small for my age. That's why everybody calls me kid."

"I heard that one before. You got working papers?"

"Sure, but they're at home. I left in kind of a hurry."

He looked me over some more. "Okay," he said finally. "Ten bucks a week. You can sleep back here and keep an eye on the place. You been a porter before?"

"Sure, for Herbie Aronowitz." I hoped he'd tell me what I was supposed to do.

But he didn't. Instead he took a key out of his pocket. "Okay. Here's the front door key. Make damn sure you keep the place locked." He handed me the key, and then he took out a roll of bills and stripped off a couple of singles. "Get me some coffee and a couple of hard rolls." He turned to leave and then turned back. "Get yourself something while you're at it."

So that was how my new life started. I'd get up around the middle of the morning, depending on how late I managed to keep myself up the night before. I'd start off feeling rotten—lonely and homesick. But I'd decided that it was worth feeling homesick if it meant I was going to be a musician. I could stand it; and I figured as time went by I'd get over it. So I'd go out for coffee and custard pie—I'd switched to pie instead of doughnuts. That would cheer me up. I'd go back to the Charleston, wash up the glasses from the night before, take out the garbage, swab the tables down, mop the floor, maybe wash out a few of the tablecloths if they were in bad shape. I'd practice for three or four hours until it was time to go out to Tommy's. We'd head off somewhere to hear one of the bands. Sometimes we'd go up to Friar's Inn to hear the Rhythm Kings, but mostly we went to the South Side—things were cheaper there, and Tommy liked Chinese food for his supper. Then we'd go over to the job. I'd bus for the waiters—empty out ashtrays when they got full, clean up the tables after a party left. Busing wasn't really part of my job, but it was something to do to keep myself awake, and an excuse to hang around the bandstand. Sometimes, if the crowd was small, Tommy'd let me sit in for a few numbers here and there to rest his lip. Between one thing and another I was getting in a lot of playing time, and hearing a lot of jazz. I was learning tunes, too. I'd sing along to a band under my breath until I got the tune pretty well memorized, and then learn it on my cornet when I was practicing. I ought to be able to play a tune in any key, Tommy told me. "Mostly they play things in standard keys, but you never can tell when you'll run into a situation where you got to play in some key you never played it in before—D-flat, E, something like that." So I learned every tune in three or four keys, so as to get the hang of different keys. I was improving a lot.

To be honest, a lot of it had to do with keeping myself busy so I didn't have time to feel homesick. It was awful hard to get rid of that feeling. I was usually all right when I was hanging around the South Side with Tommy, or sitting in with his outfit at the Charleston. It was hard to feel bad with that music going in a room full of people having a good time for themselves. And by the time I turned in I could hardly keep my eyes open and didn't have any trouble falling asleep.

But then would come morning. I'd wake up in that cellar with a clear view of the coal bin and the stink of old beer in my nose, and I'd miss home so bad I'd like to bust out crying. I'd remember sitting at our old kitchen table talking with Ma about nothing special while she cooked. I'd remember how Pa went around the table at suppertime asking everybody how things had gone that day—did John get his Shakespeare report in, did I pass my math test, did Ma get over to see Grampa? I knew I shouldn't dwell on old memories, I had a new life now, and none of that mattered anymore. But I couldn't help myself. It comforted me some to remember things like that. I kept looking forward to the time when I'd made a go of it as a musician, had a few bucks in my pocket, and could walk in on them dressed in brand-new clothes—maybe a midnight blue overcoat like the one Calvin Wilson had. That'd be something all right, to come marching in on them togged out like a swell.

How long would it be before I could do that? Tommy figured I was pretty near ready to branch out on my own. The problem was that I still looked like a kid. It worked against me, Tommy said. Jazz musicians were mostly pretty young as it was—eighteen, twenty, twenty-three. They didn't want to make matters worse by bringing a real kid up on the stand. But I was growing fast. I figured in a year I'd look a good deal older, and if I dressed up a bit, and maybe grew a mustache, if I could, I'd get away with it.

I decided to set my sights on that: a year to the day after I ran away I'd walk back in there togged out like a swell, with my own job behind me and a few bucks in my pocket. In the meantime I'd keep myself as busy as I could and hope that the homesickness would wear off.

I scratched my way through a week or so like this, getting a little more used to it. Then one afternoon when I was mopping the floor the door opened, and in came Herbie Aronowitz. It made me jump to see him. He stood there by the door in his blue suit, one hand on the doorjamb. "Where's Silva?" he said.

"He doesn't usually come in until later," I said. It made me plenty nervous to see him.

"I didn't ask that. I asked where he was."

"I don't know," I said. "He never tells me where he's going. I'm just the porter here. I don't even know where he lives." Herbie didn't seem to recognize me.

He didn't say anything for a minute, just stood there looking around. "Do pretty good business here?" he said finally.

"Sometimes good. Sometimes it's pretty quiet."

He looked around some more, taking everything in. Then he said, "You tell Silva that Herbie was looking for him." He gave me a hard look. "You got me?"

"Yes, sir," I said.

"Tell him Herb wants to see him."

"Yes, sir."

He turned to go. Then he turned back and stared at me some more. "Don't I know you from somewhere?"

I got hot and scratched my head. "Maybe you saw me here before."

He shook his head. "Ain't you the plumber's kid? Frank Horvath's kid?"

"Naw," I said, trying to look at him straight on. "My pa died a long time ago. He worked in the stockyards."

He went on looking at me. "You sure you ain't Frank Horvath's kid? The kid that came around once looking for a wrench that wasn't there?"

"I wished I was," I said. "I wished I was somebody's kid instead of sleeping in that back room next to the coal bin."

"Well, you look like him." He started to go out, and then turned back once more. "Make sure you give Silva the message. Herbie wants to see him."

I had sense enough to wait until I caught Mr. Silva alone before I gave him the message. He took his tan fedora off, held it by the brim with both hands, and stood there frowning at it, as if there was an answer to some question in it. "That all Herb said? He wants to see me? He didn't say what it was about?"

"That's all. Just that he wants to see you."

Mr. Silva didn't say anything, but went on staring into the hat. Then he remembered I was standing there. "Yeah, I know what it was. It ain't nothing important." He stared into the hat some more, and then he remembered me again. "You go on back to work," he said.

I didn't know what it was about and I didn't want to know. It was Mr. Silva's problem. I was much more worried that Herb would run into Pa and drop it to him that he'd seen a kid that looked like me. It didn't seem likely that it would come up. I wasn't of any importance to Herbie Aronowitz; why would he bother to keep me in mind?

On the other side of it, Pa *would* bother to keep me in mind. He'd have a pretty good idea that I was liable to be hanging around jazz joints. If he ran into Herbie he might ask him to keep an eye out for me, and of course Herbie would put two and two together. Maybe I ought to get out of there. Maybe I ought to find a job portering somewhere else.

I hated to do that. For one thing, where would I sleep until I found a new joint? For another, it was mighty comforting to see Tommy Hurd all the time. He was familiar to me. I decided to take a chance on it. Probably Herb had forgotten all about me the minute he walked out of the place.

15

TWO DAYS LATER something happened that made me glad I was busing tables in Silva's club. Tommy's band was on the stand, playing, I was clearing up after a party that had just gone out, when in came about six people. At least two of them were musicians, for they were carrying instrument cases. They'd probably just got off their own jobs and were going around to the after-hours joints to hear what was going on, and maybe sit in. The others looked like the type of jazz fan that followed their favorite musicians around all night, just to be part of things.

They stood there waiting for me to finish clearing the table. One of them, a kind of big, athletic-looking fella, had a cornet case. His bow tie was undone, his collar unbuttoned. I finished swabbing off the table and went into the kitchen with the dirty ashtray. When I came back they were sitting at the table. The cornet player had his feet up on a chair, and was leaning back, listening to the band. I came over with the clean ashtray. Just then Tommy took the band out with a two-bar tag. He hopped off the bandstand and trotted over to the table. "Bix," he said. "It's swell to see you. Come on up and play."

It was Bix Beiderbecke. I stood there polishing up the ashtray with my apron. Bix shook his head. "Naw, you guys are too good for me."

The fans around the table laughed. "Come on, Bix," Tommy said.

"Well, I might be encouraged if I had a drink." They all laughed again, even though it wasn't really funny. I went on polishing the ashtray.

"Kid, get Bix a drink." I went into the kitchen and fixed the drink. By the time I got back Bix was up on the bandstand, flapping the valves of his cornet. I brought the drink over, handed it to him, and then stepped over to the side of the bandstand where I wouldn't miss anything. The busing could wait.

"What do you want to do, Bix?"

He shrugged, took a swallow of whiskey, and set the glass down by his feet. "China Boy?"

Tommy nodded and stomped the band off. He stood back a little letting Bix take the lead and filling in behind. And oh my, wasn't it something? It was like Tommy had said: Bix had a way of playing like nobody else, a style that was all his own. He wasn't running all over the horn the way Louie did, high F's all over the place. He kept to the middle, banging out the notes exactly so, sharp and precise, with a clean, warm sound. I could see right away what his idea of improvising was—sew together little ideas so that you could see the sense of them as they came along one after another. He wasn't just tossing notes out there to fit the chord changes, the way a lot of guys did. The ideas linked up, one after the other, into a long chain that was solid as iron. It was different from Louie's way of playing: where Louie was always telling a big story of some kind, Bix was making little poems. You could almost hear the rhymes.

It took my breath away. I stood there hardly able to move through three numbers, until I saw Mr. Silva by the kitchen door giving me a look, and went back to busing again. But I knew I'd have to find a way of hearing Bix again, for in twenty minutes he'd showed me a whole lot about jazz I never understood before.

I talked with Tommy about it later. "Do you think he's better than Louie Armstrong?" Calvin had told us his full name.

Tommy shrugged. "Who's to say what better is? They got different styles."

"Yeah," I said. "But you know what I mean."

"Some people think Bix is tops, some people would take Louie. Oliver ain't too bad, either. What about Phil Napoleon with the Memphis Five bunch?

What about Mares? You got a whole lot to choose from."

"Tommy, don't you think that Bix has a prettier sound than Louie? Maybe I ought to try to get that sound."

He gave me a look. "Kid, that ain't the point. It's not how to get Bix or Louie into it. The point is how to get yourself into it, how to make it sound like you. Point is, how do *you* want it to sound? First you got to figure out what *you* want to play, or you can't do nothing."

It all gave me an awful lot to think about. Tommy was right. I could see that you had to get a piece of yourself into the music. But how did you do that? Who was I anyway? I was sitting in the furnace room one afternoon fooling around with the cornet, just trying this and that to see if I was getting my-self into it, when suddenly the door opened and Herbie Aronowitz was standing there. His overcoat was unbuttoned, and I could see his usual blue suit, no tie.

I dropped the cornet onto the cot and jumped up. "Mr. Silva isn't here."

He stared at me for a minute. "No, I was looking for you, Paulie."

"Paulie? My name is Johnny—"

He laughed. "Don't hand me none of that, Paulie. I thought it was you all along."

I was stuck. "How'd you know?"

"From your pa. He came around asking me if you

turned up at any of my clubs. He figured you was likely to be tagging around after Tommy Hurd."

"Oh." I felt sick. "Did you tell Pa where I was?"

"No," he said. "Not yet, anyways. I might and I might not."

"Yes, sir," I said. Would he do anything to me for lying to him?

He looked at me for a while, not blinking. "When does Silva usually come in?"

I was plenty scared, and didn't dare lie to him.

"Usually around ten, to unlock the liquor. The waiters come in at eleven to set up. The band starts at midnight."

"Where's Silva usually at?"

"By the door, keeping an eye on who's coming in," I said. I wished I didn't have to tell him all this stuff, but I was too scared not to.

"He got someone with him?"

I shook my head. "One of the waiters is pretty big. He can handle anyone who makes trouble."

"What time he close up?"

"Depends. Usually the place is empty by six and we close, but you can't be sure."

He reached into his trousers pocket, pulled out a fat roll of bills, and unrolled a ten. "Here," he said. "Get yourself a pair of long pants. I don't want nobody in knee pants working for me." Then he was gone.

I sat down on the cot, feeling mighty shaky. The

last thing I ever wanted was to get involved with gangsters. How could I get out of it? What was I going to tell Angelo Silva? Had he done something to Herb? Were they taking over his joint? I remember what Calvin Wilson had said about Herbie Aronowitz treading on people's toes. Maybe that was the whole thing—they wanted to take over the Charleston. But maybe it was something worse.

I lay down on the cot and stared at the ceiling. What a mess I was getting myself into. Living all by myself in a furnace room next to a coal bin, coffee and pie for breakfast, chop suey every night for supper. Giving myself a bath as best I could out of the sink in the kitchen. No one to talk to all day long. I'd given everything up for jazz, and where had it got me? Mixed up with the gangsters. Running away from Ma and Pa was one thing; running away from the gangsters would be a lot harder, for they were everywhere in Chicago, and you never even knew who they were.

I had to talk to Tommy. He came in a few minutes late and had to go right on the stand; and during the first break a party of good tippers wanted him to have a drink with them, so it wasn't until the second break that I could get him outside for a few minutes. "Let's walk down to the corner," I said.

"What's going on, kid?"

"I'll tell you in a minute," I said. I waited until we were a half a block away from the club. "Herb Aronowitz came around today. They're after Silva."

Tommy stopped walking and looked at me. "What'd Herbie say?"

"Nothing straight out. He just wanted to know what time Silva came in, where he was during the night, when he closed the place."

Tommy took a look up and down the street. It was pretty quiet, just a couple of people out. "Come on, let's walk," he said. After a bit he said, "It doesn't sound good, does it."

"What should I do?"

"Do? Don't do nothing, kid. Stay out of it."

"Don't I have to tell Silva?" I said. "Don't I have to warn him?"

"You don't have to do nothing of the kind, kid. What you got to do is stay clear of the whole thing. The gangsters own Chi, lock, stock, and barrel. You get in wrong with them, you might as well leave town. Musicians don't mean nothing to them. Just as soon shoot one as shoot a duck. You get in trouble with the gangs you might as well chuck your cornet in the river."

"What do you think they'll do to Silva?"

Tommy shrugged. "Who knows. Push him around a little, maybe. Maybe worse. It ain't any of our business."

"But suppose they're planning to kill him," I said. "I have to warn him, don't I?"

"You stay the hell out of it. You haven't got no idea what Silva was up to. He ain't any better than the rest. Maybe he's just going to get what he deserves."

"What if they take over the club? Will you lose the job?"

Tommy shrugged again. "Who knows? Something else'll turn up. There's plenty of work around Chi. Better to sit home for a week than get in trouble with the gangsters." He nodded his head towards the club. "I got to get back."

"Tommy, Herbie gave me ten dollars and told me to buy long pants. What if Silva suspects something?"

"Tell him I gave you the dough. Tell him I got sick of seeing you around in knee pants. Come on. I got to get back."

16

SOMETIMES I DIDN'T wait for the club to empty out before I went to bed. I still wasn't used to staying up all night, the way Tommy was. He'd worked after-hours joints an awful lot, and night was day for him. At an after-hours club the job usually finished by six or so. Tommy'd go off with some of the boys in the band for a meal—usually eggs, bacon, pancakes was what you could get at that hour. If it wasn't too late they'd get somebody who had a car and go for a drive out into the country. Or play golf. The piano player was nuts about golf and Tommy'd go along with him. They were all worried about their lungs, especially the horn players. Everybody had stories about musicians whose lungs went from spending too much time in dives breathing cigarette smoke. They figured fresh air would clean their lungs out, so they'd play golf, go for a drive, or swim in the lake if the weather was okay. It was a funny way to live, playing golf at eight o'clock in the morning when everybody else was crowded on streetcars headed for factories and offices. I liked the idea of it. It was the way I meant to live, once I got myself going in music. But I wasn't used to it yet. I'd generally manage to keep myself going until four or five, when there wasn't likely to be more than one or two parties left in the club. Then I'd turn in. I could clean up after the last parties when I got up.

A couple of nights after Aronowitz had come around asking questions about Silva, I went to bed at around five. Silva was sitting at a table with a party, and the band was loafing its way through the last set—taking long pauses between numbers and playing a lot of slow ballads. By this time of night they were usually pretty beat.

I kicked off my shoes, lay down on the cot, pulled the army blanket over me, and fell asleep. Sometime later noises began to filter through my dreams and after a while I slid out of sleep. For a minute I lay there trying to figure out what was a dream and what wasn't. The sun was shining through the high window, which meant that it was around nine or ten o'clock, for the sun moved off that side of the building by the middle of the morning. I shook my head; and then I realized there were voices coming from the club. I sat up, listening.

"You been a naughty boy, Angelo. You know what happens to naughty boys."

"I swear I never did it, Herbie," Silva said. He sounded scared all right. "I wouldn't do nothing like that to you, Herb. Who told you I did it?"

"A little birdy told me."

"Herbie, you got to believe me," Silva said. "I never did it."

There was a little silence. I sat there waiting, my heart pounding in my chest. "Socks, see if you can get Angelo to come clean."

"Hey—" There was a thump. "Jesus," Silva cried. "Go easy, Socks."

The thump came again and then the sound of a chair rattling to the floor. There was another silence and then Silva said, kind of slow, "You want the club, Herbie? Is that it? Take the club, with my blessings. It's yours. I'll just walk out of here."

"Not yet, Angelo. I ain't finished with you yet."

I had to get out of there. What if they came into the back room and found me sitting there listening to the whole thing? My hands were damp and there was sweat dripping from my forehead. I wiped my face off with my sleeve. Could I squeeze through that little window? What if I got stuck halfway through?

Out in the club Silva said, "Please, Herbie, have mercy. I never did it." There was another thump, and the clatter of an ashtray hitting the floor. I stood up off the bed as quiet as I could, picked up my shoes, and took my jacket off the nail in the wall. I tiptoed across the room, my shoes in one hand, my jacket in the other. My cornet was out in the club by the bandstand. It made me sick to think of losing that Selmer. Maybe Tommy could get it for me if I ever got out of this.

Out in the club there came a shriek. "Socks, you're gonna break my arm." I reached the back wall, put my jacket on the floor, and with my free hand unlatched the window. I swung it down toward me. It gave off a squeal, for it hadn't been opened for a long time. I stopped, holding it halfway open. From out in the club there came a snapping noise. Silva shrieked. "You busted it, Socks. You busted my arm."

I lowered the window all the way. It made a good loud squeal. I flung my shoes and jacket into the alley. From the club I heard Herbie say, "What the hell was that?" I grabbed hold of the windowsill, heaved myself up, and shoved my head and shoulders through.

"Go see what that noise was, Socks. I'll keep an eye on Angelo."

I pulled myself through the window and out into the alley. Behind me I heard the door to the furnace room open. A voice shouted, "Hey, you." I grabbed my shoes and jacket and ran in my stockings down the cold dirt of the alley. I didn't look back, but kept on running. When I hit the street I turned left, away from the club, and ran on. There were a lot of people out, and they stared at me running along the sidewalk in my stockings, carrying my shoes and jacket, but I didn't dare stop to put them on. I prayed I wouldn't run into a cop, for he was bound to think I'd stolen the jacket. I came to the corner, swung around it, ran on up the block, across the street and down another side street. Here, finally, I stopped, panting and soaked with sweat, and looked back.

Nobody was coming that I could see. Quickly I knelt, put on my shoes, stood up and put on my jacket, already running again while I buttoned it. As I came out onto the avenue I saw a streetcar coming along. I jumped on, had another look behind me, and then squirmed into the middle of the streetcar where the crowd was thick. I'd got away—but everything I'd worked for was lost.

I took the streetcar as far as Madison and got off. I didn't even have to think where I was going. There was only one place, and I went there, walking along as quick as I could, scared and lonely and looking around all the time, just in case.

When I got to Tommy's it was five of ten, according to the clock in the drugstore across the street. Tommy wasn't even home yet. Would Herb Aronowitz figure out I was likely to go to Tommy's? I went around the corner and leaned against a building where I could see the stoop to Tommy's boarding house. For a good half hour I waited there, and then I saw Tommy coming slowly up the street in his old brown overcoat, his cornet case in his hand. I waited until he was nearly at the stoop and darted out. "Tommy," I called.

He looked up. "Hey, kid. What're you doing here?"

"I'm in real trouble. Herbie is looking for me." I looked around.

He looked around to see what I was looking for. "What the hell for?"

"I'll tell you. Let's get off the street." We went up to Tommy's little room, with the records scattered around the floor and clothes lying on a chair. We sat side by side on the bed and I told him the whole story—about Angelo Silva getting his arm busted, and me climbing out the window just as the gangster was coming into the furnace room.

"Maybe he didn't see you. How could he tell who was going out the window when all he could see was a couple of legs?"

"Who else would they think it was?"

"Silva knows you was sleeping in there, but how would Herbie know? It could have been some waiter, anybody as far as those guys knew."

"I can't take a chance on it. Herbie's going to take over the joint. When I don't turn up tonight they'll know for sure it was me who overheard them. If they ended up killing Silva they'll want to make sure I don't squeal on them."

Tommy didn't say anything for a while. Then he said, "Maybe I can find out something. I have to be damn careful, though. I can't let on that I know anything."

"What'll you do tonight?"

"Just go in as usual and play, like I don't know nothing about it. I'll see what I'll see. Who knows, maybe they just roughed Silva up a little. Maybe he'll be by the door as usual with his arm in a sling and some story about spraining his wrist when he was cranking his car."

"What should I do, Tommy?"

He was quiet again. Then he said, "Maybe you should go home."

"How can I do that? Once Herbie sees I'm not working at the club anymore, he's bound to go around to Pa's house to see if I'm there."

"I thought your pa was a pal of Herb's. Couldn't he put in a good word?"

I remembered the way they'd pushed Pa around. "He's not that much of a pal."

"I still think you ought to go home, kid. Let your pa work it out somehow. Maybe send you out of town for a while. You got relatives downstate, ain't you?"

"Please, Tommy. See what you can find out tonight."

"Okay. I'll try." He shook his head. "I always figured I had 'em beat for getting myself in messes, but you take the cake. You better hole up here tonight."

"What if they come looking for me?"

It ain't likely. I'll lock you in when I go out. Better go out and get yourself a couple of sandwiches to tide you over."

So I went around the corner to the greasy spoon,

ate a ham sandwich even though I wasn't hungry, and brought another one home. Tommy was already asleep when I got back. I snuggled down in his beat-up easy chair and went to sleep myself. I slept through to the middle of the afternoon, and woke up feeling nervous and queasy in my stomach. I wished I dared go for a walk so as not to feel so nervous, but I didn't. Finally Tommy woke up. We chewed the fat for a little while. Then he said he had a date and was going to the steam baths to clean up first. "If anyone knocks, climb out the window and go down the fire escape." Then he left. I heard the key turn in the lock.

After that there was nothing to do but wait. I sat on the floor playing records for a while, until I remembered that anybody out in the hall could hear the music and would know somebody was there. My heart wasn't in it, anyway. I read a couple of old dime westerns Tommy had lying around and finally, around ten o'clock, I turned off the lights and lay down on Tommy's bed. I didn't think I'd be able to sleep, for I'd gotten used to staying up late; but by and by I dozed off, and slept through until Tommy came in at eight o'clock, carrying coffee and pastrami sandwiches.

"Well, you was right, kid. Herbie thinks it was you in there."

"What did he say? Is he taking over the club?"

"Looks like it," Tommy said. "Silva wasn't nowhere to be seen. Herb said Silva had an accident and asked Herb to cover for him at the club. Everything was to go on normal."

"Do you think they killed him?"

He thought about it. "Probably not. They didn't have to. Probably just busted him up enough so's he'd be out of circulation for a while."

"And he knows it was me who was going out the window."

"Yeah, I guess he does. He came around after the second set and said, 'Where's the kid?' I said I didn't know, but that Silva told me he caught you stealing liquor last week and was going to can you. I don't know as he believed it."

"Why wouldn't he believe it?"

"He saw your cornet case sitting there. He said, 'Isn't that the kid's horn?' I said, 'No, it's mine, I was lending it to the kid.' He said, 'Well leave it sit there for a while.' "

"Boy, am I in a mess."

Tommy didn't say anything for a bit, but chewed off a bite of the pastrami sandwich. Finally he said, "Kid, I hate to tell you this, but you got worse trouble than you think. Herbie thinks your pa had something to do with it."

"Pa? He thinks that? Why would Pa have anything to do with it?"

"He told me that once, a while back, your pa sent you around to that other club where we was playing, with some cock-and-bull story about looking for a wrench. He said, 'Frankie Horvath is up to something. If you see the kid, tell him I want to talk to him.' "

"Pa didn't have anything to do with it," I cried. "I made that whole story up myself so's to get in there and hear you guys."

Tommy nodded. "Knowing you, I can believe it. It's just the thing you'd do. But that ain't the way Herbie sees it. You got to remember, these here gangsters don't trust nobody or nothing. They see some old pooch sniffing around the place, they take it for a cop. That's what it's like being a gangster. You sit with your back to the wall all the time, sleep with one eye open and a machine gun for a pillow. A guy like Herb Aronowitz has got more money than most banks, and nobody messes with him. But I wouldn't want to be him for all the tea in China. He can't take a woman out to dinner without worrying she's going to double-cross him to the cops, he can't take his dog for a walk after dinner without worrying there's somebody down behind every bush drawing a bead on him. It don't take very much to get him suspicious of somebody."

"What do you think he might try to do to Pa?"

Tommy shrugged and finished off his sandwich. "I couldn't even guess."

"But Pa didn't have anything to do with any of it."

"It ain't no use telling me that," Tommy said. "I already believe you."

I sat there thinking. "What am I going to do, Tommy?"

"Well, like I said, hide out for a while. Go visit your people downstate for a few months. These things blow over. In a few months Herb'll have six other people he's suspicious of and will have forgotten all about you."

"What about Pa?"

"That's something you got to decide for yourself, kid."

"What a mess," I said. "How did I manage to get myself so messed up, Tommy?"

He sat there thinking and licking the grease off his fingers for a while. Then he said, "Well, I'll tell you, kid, I done the same thing myself a few times. What it comes out of is thinking you just *got* to have a certain thing, no matter what. You won't let nothing stand in your way and you go barreling after it, without seeing how it might go wrong. It comes over you so hot it doesn't matter what you have to do to get it. Lie, cheat, steal—it all seems okay in your mind. Next thing you know you got a lion by the tail."

"I never stole," I said.

"Sure you did. You borrowed that seventy-five cents off your brother and never had no intention of paying it back."

"I paid it back." But I couldn't remember if I had or not.

"Now mind you," Tommy said, "I ain't blaming you. I did all the same stuff myself. Worse. I stole the first decent cornet I ever owned."

"You stole it?"

"Out of a pawnshop. It was in the window, new and shiny. I don't doubt but what it was stole in the first place. I was playing an old beat-up piece of tin I rented from school. Leaked like a sieve. You could hear the air coming out of the valves every time you blew it. St. Peter hisself couldn't of played it in tune. That cornet in the pawnshop window drove me crazy. I used to go around there every day, just to look at it. Just stand for a half an hour and look at it. One night I heaved a rock through the window, snatched the horn out of there and ran like the wind. Well, naturally the guy in the pawnshop knew in a minute who stole it. If I'd had any brains I'd of taken some other stuff, too, but when he saw it was only the cornet, he went around the neighborhood looking for me. I wasn't hard to find, for everybody knew who the damn kid was who kept them awake tootling that horn at all hours. The cops caught me at home red-handed. The judge said it was either reform school, or a hundred-dollar fine. That was the time Pa couldn't work because of his bad leg, and we needed the money I was making. Sis went out and got the hundred bucks. I don't know where she got it, and I never asked. And on top of it, I was back playing that leaky piece of tin all over again. That's the way it is when you get so stuck on something you can't see anything else—you ain't the only one who gets hurt."

"So you think I did wrong right from the beginning?"

He shook his head. "I didn't say that. It ain't up to me to say if anybody's right or wrong. You got to settle that out for yourself."

I hung my head down and sat there thinking. Outside horns honked faintly, and trucks ground down the street. Finally Tommy said, "I got to get some sleep, kid."

17 GETTING MYSELF TO admit that they were right and I was wrong was about the hardest thing I ever did. I didn't want to admit it—I hated having to do that, and for a long time I sat there in Tommy's chair while he snoozed in bed, thinking of all the arguments on my side of it. Why was it my fault that Herbie Aronowitz had got suspicious of Pa for no reason? Why was it my fault I fell in love with some kind of music Ma and Pa hated? Why should Pa have the say about how I lived my life—that I had to spend my days in the plumbing business and no choice left to me? What was right about that?

They were all good arguments. But they weren't good enough. It was the way Tommy said. I'd gone steaming off on my own without looking down the road to see what might come of it, and I'd got Pa in trouble. It didn't matter that I had a right to steam off on my own; what mattered was that Pa was in trouble for something I'd done. What was going to happen to my music? I didn't know; I'd have to worry about that later.

Had Herbie Aronowitz already gone looking for Pa? There was no telling. How much of a chance did I have of persuading Herb that Pa didn't have anything to do with it? No telling about that, either. But I'd got Pa into it, and it was up to me to get him out. Oh, that was a mighty scary idea, for there was no telling what Herbie might do to me, either. But I had to try.

The safest thing, I figured, was to go over to the Charleston a little before midnight. Normally I would have been there earlier, but I figured Herbie wouldn't know that. I'd walk in like everything was normal, and maybe it would be. Maybe Herbie would have cooled down a little and turned his mind to something else. But if he hadn't, by midnight the waiters would already be there. I figured Herbie wouldn't get rough with me with the waiters around.

I killed some time at a movie, but it didn't help much, for I couldn't concentrate on the picture. All I could think was, why me? How come it was me who had got into this mess? Why wasn't it happening to somebody else? I knew that what Tommy had said was right—I'd plunged ahead towards what I wanted, and ended up running off a cliff. Still, the words kept going through my head: Why me? Why wasn't it happening to somebody else?

At ten to twelve I left the movie theater and walked over to the Charleston, wishing I was going anywhere else. I just kept putting one foot in front of the next, and by and by I was there. For a minute I stood outside, hoping that something would happen to save me. But it didn't. I took a deep breath and went on in.

One of the waiters was sweeping the floor, and the other was in the kitchen washing glasses, for of course I hadn't been there to clean the place up that morning. The one sweeping gave me a look when I came in. "Where the hell was you?" he said.

Herbie Aronowitz was sitting at a table with a cashbox in front of him, counting money. When the waiter spoke, he looked up. "Well. The kid."

"I'm sorry I let you down the last couple of nights, Mr. Aronowitz," I said. "My Grampa's mighty sick and I went over to see him."

"Yeah? Tommy tell you I wanted to see you?"

"I haven't seen Tommy for a couple of days. I was over at my Grampa's. They don't think he'll last."

"Oh yeah?" Herbie said. "Well give your ma my condolences."

"Grampa hasn't died yet."

He looked back at the cashbox. "Give 'em to her anyway." He started counting money again, laying it out in neat piles of bills. I headed for the kitchen to get a mop. "Hold up a minute, kid," Herbie said. "I wanna talk to you. Go out back and wait for me."

For a couple of seconds I thought of making a dash for the front door, but of course that wasn't the point of the whole thing. So I turned, went out into the furnace room, shut the door behind me, and sat down on the cot. Sweat was dripping out of my armpits and rolling in cold drops down my side, and my stomach was like ice. I just went on sitting there. By and by I heard a scale run down the piano. In a couple of minutes a bass drum thumped: the drummer was tightening the skin and testing the sound. Finally there came that old familiar warm-up phrase on the cornet, the one I first heard in that cold cellar—was it really two years ago? And in a moment they were playing "Whispering," a tune Tommy liked to open with, for it was easy and a hit with people.

Then the door to the furnace room opened. Herbie came in. He'd been waiting until the music started so as to cover sounds from the furnace room. He shut the door behind him, and stood there in that same blue suit, no tie, looking at me. There was no expression on his face; he just stared. Then he said, "C'mere, kid." I stood up off the cot and took a couple of steps toward him, still far enough away so he couldn't reach me.

"Kid, you're getting too big for your britches. You and your pa."

Out in the club the piano was soloing. "Pa didn't

have anything to do with it. Honest. I made up that whole story about the wrench myself, so I could get in to hear the band. I wanted Tommy to give me lessons."

He shook his head. "I don't want to hear nothing about no lessons. What's your game, kid?" He squinted at me. "What're you and your pa up to?"

"Honest, we don't have any game." I was sweating everywhere I could sweat, skin getting soaked. How could I make him believe me? "It's the truth. I made up that whole story about the wrench myself. Pa didn't know anything about it. When he found out he belted me."

Suddenly he lunged forward and grabbed me by the shirtfront with his big hand. "Don't give me none of that. You tell me what your game is, or I'll beat the living Jesus out of you. What was you doing climbing out of that window the other morning?"

"Honest—" I started to say it wasn't me. Then I realized he'd know I was lying and wouldn't believe anything I said. "I was scared. I didn't want to hear anything that wasn't my business."

He had his hand cocked back to whack me, but he realized I was probably telling the truth, and held up. For a minute he didn't say anything, but stood there with his fist cocked. He blinked a couple of times. "What was it you thought you heard?"

I looked up into his face. "Angelo Silva said his arm was broken."

Herbie lowered his fist. "Naw," he said. "Angelo

and me is old pals. I wouldn't of let nobody lay a finger on him. You don't believe a story like that, do you, kid?"

I shook my head as hard as I could. "No, sir. If you said it wasn't true I wouldn't believe it."

He went on holding me by the shirt. "That's right, kid. Angelo took sick. He'll be laid up for a while. He asked me as a favor to look after the club for him."

"Yes, sir."

"But there's something I still don't get. What kind of a game is Frankie Horvath playing?" He raised his fist. "Has he got big ideas or something?"

The sweat was soaking into my clothes. Now, out in the club, Tommy was taking his solo. "Honest, it's all a mistake. Pa doesn't know anything about it. He doesn't even know I've been working here. He doesn't know where I am."

"You just told me you was visiting your Grampa." He opened his hand to slap me.

"That was a lie," I said. "I was too scared to come in." I didn't want to bring Tommy into it. "I've been sleeping at the railroad station."

He shook his head. "You tell a lot of lies, don't you kid."

"I swear this is the truth. Pa doesn't know where I am."

He stood there looking at me, with his palm raised. In the club the band was playing the final chorus of "Whispering." He shook his head again. "Kid, I guess I got to beat it out of you."

"Please," I said. "It's the truth." The band played a tag, and the music stopped. So did Herbie's hand. He scowled, and turned his head to look at the door. But instead of music, there was a knock. "Who the hell's that?"

"It's me, Herbie. Tommy."

"What'd you want? Go play another tune."

"Herbie, there's a fella here to see you."

"I don't want to see nobody. Tell him to come back later."

There was a little silence. "I figured you'd want to know. He says he's the kid's pa." Then the door opened, and Pa came in. "Hello, Herb," he said.

It was an almighty shock seeing Pa come through the door like that. I stood there feeling confused, my feelings coming and going so fast I couldn't catch hold of them—ashamed for him having to get me out of trouble after I'd run off, relieved that I'd been saved from being smacked around, worried about what would happen to him. How was he going to explain to Herbie that we weren't up to anything.

"Pa—"

"Shut the door, Frankie," Herb said.

Pa jerked his head at me. "Herb, you don't have to start knocking a kid around. You want to talk to somebody, you can talk to me."

Herbie let go of my shirtfront. "Yeah, that's right, Frankie. I can talk to you."

"Paulie," Pa said. "You go on home. Your ma's waiting for you."

There wasn't anything I wanted more than to go home. But I didn't want to leave Pa in trouble.

"Pa, I never—"

"Paulie, I said go home."

I slipped past them and out into the club. Tommy was on the stand, blowing water out of his spit valve. I gave him a little wave. Then I dashed through the club and headed for home. So it was over for now. I'd have to admit I was wrong, and say I was sorry—no way around that. And I was sorry, too, the way things worked out. But I wasn't going to admit I was wrong about my music. Wrong about steaming off on my own and getting Pa into trouble. But not wrong about my music—I'd never admit I was wrong about that.

Ma and John were sitting in the kitchen at the old wooden table, just sitting there, waiting. When I came through the door, they stood up. I didn't know if they hated me or were glad to see me, or what. But I was sure glad to see them.

For a minute nobody said anything: they looked at me and I looked at them. But I knew what I had to do. "I'm sorry, Ma. I'm sorry I caused everybody so much trouble."

"I should think you would be," Ma said. But she put her hands over her eyes and rubbed at them, like they were tired. "When on earth was the last time you washed that shirt?"

I took out my handkerchief and blew my nose.

"Where the hell have you been?" John said. He

sounded sore, but I knew he was plenty curious—maybe jealous, too, that I'd had some adventure he was left out of.

"John," Ma said, "It isn't up to you to chastise Paulie. That's Pa's business. Paulie, sit down. There's some leftover stew. I'll heat it up for you."

I sat down. "How did Pa find me? How did he know where I was?"

"Your friend Tommy came over about an hour ago. He said you'd been at his place, but was gone, and he was worried that you'd gone over to that dive. He and Pa went over. Pa was going to wait outside while your friend found out if you were there."

I could see what had happened. When Tommy came in Herbie had still been out in the club. He'd told Tommy to start playing. I figured that during the piano solo Tommy had walked off the bandstand and asked one of the waiters if I was there. Then he'd signaled to Pa somehow, as soon as he got a chance. Something like that, anyway.

But I didn't know for sure, and I wasn't going to find out that night, for as soon as I finished a bowl of stew Ma said we'd all lost enough sleep over me as it was, and we were going to bed.

We didn't get to talk about it until supper the next night, for Pa wasn't about to miss a day's work, no matter what, and I wasn't in the habit of waking up until noon. But Pa came home early. We all sat down in the living room, and Pa made me tell them the whole story—where I'd been, what I'd done, how I managed to feed myself. I told it all.

When I got done they all sat back and looked at me. Then Pa said, "What made you do a damn fool thing like going back to that club last night?"

I shrugged. "I figured I'd try to explain to Herbie that you didn't have anything to do with it."

He shook his head. "That took guts, Paulie. I got to admit it. I just wished you had some brains to go along with it."

"How did it come out with Herb?" That was still the worrisome thing.

"It might have been worse if he had one of his pals around—that guy Socks, or somebody. But he wasn't expecting me, and he had figured he could handle you himself. I cut a deal with him. I told him I'd see you kept your mouth shut." He stared at me. "You understand that, Paulie? You don't tell nobody anything—not Rory Flynn, not anybody."

"Yes. I understand."

"That's not all, Paulie. Herbie owed me two hundred seventy-five bucks. I told him I'd call it quits between him and me, even-steven."

"Two hundred and seventy-five dollars?"

Pa nodded. "That's a lot of money, Paulie. Think about what this family could do with that much money. I could buy your ma a nice used car for that. We could get a new living room suite. There's a lot of things we could have done with that money. Think about it, Paulie."

It was just what had happened to Tommy—got his heart set on that pawnshop cornet, and in the end it cost his sis a hundred bucks. All three of them were staring at me, to see if the message was taking hold. I felt pretty rotten. I looked at them, and then looked down at the carpet. "I'm sorry. It's all my fault." I looked up again, hoping somebody would say it wasn't.

Pa shook his head. "No, Paulie, it isn't *all* your fault. I'm to blame some, too. Where I made my mistake was to get involved with Herb Aronowitz in the first place. It was easy money. Good enough for everybody else, and why shouldn't I take some of it? But the chickens always come home to roost. If we hadn't been in that there club two years ago, none of this would have happened, would it?"

"Pa, I'd have found out about jazz sooner or later."

"Yeah, but it would have been later and it wouldn't have been in no gangster club. In the meanwhile, maybe you wouldn't have flunked school. I got to take part of the blame. You get mixed up with a guy like Herb, it rubs off on you sooner or later."

He looked at me, and I looked at him. "But not all of it, Paulie. You went off like you was a grown-up and got yourself in a mess. You can't have it both ways. If you're a grown-up, you stay out of messes. So long as I have to get you out of them, you gotta do what I tell you."

I didn't like that idea, but I could see the justice of it. "Yes, Pa."

He leaned back in his chair, with his arms over his head. "Now, this friend of yours, this fella Tommy."

"Tommy Hurd."

"We had a long talk with him. He came up hard, like me. He isn't as dumb as I took him for at first."

"He's real smart," I said. "But his ma died when he was young, and he didn't get much schooling."

"One thing he said stuck with me. He said, if you wasn't any good at anything but music, it didn't make much sense to keep you from it. He said there's good money in it, and you were coming along fine."

Ma bit her lip. "Paulie's going back to school."

Pa went on looking at me. "Now it cost me two-seventy-five to get you out of this. You owe me one. You're going back to school and pass a few things for your ma's sake. We'll see how it goes. And then if you're still all fired up to go into music, I won't stand in your way. No point in trying to make a plumber out of you if you're going to burn somebody's house down with a blowtorch because you was dreaming about music and set the drapes on fire."

"Pa, I promise. I'll try to pass." It seemed like I'd been saying that all my life.

"You have to try as hard as you can, Paulie," Ma said.

Well, I'd try. Probably I could manage to get out of eighth grade, at least, for I was going to be older than the others, and maybe I'd be a little smarter, too. Besides, I'd have the time for it; it'd be a while before I dared to bring up music around there. How long?

Three, four months. Maybe six months. In the meantime I could practice over at Rory's, or Tommy's— enough to keep my lip up, anyway. Tommy'd get my Selmer back for me, and I could keep it at Rory's. Then, if it looked like I was going to pass a few subjects, I'd lean on Ma to let me start practicing at home. She had a soft spot for me.

How Much of
This Book Is True?

PAULIE HORVATH AND his family are, of course, made up. So is Tommy Hurd, and the various gangsters who appear in the story. So, too, are the clubs in which Tommy is shown as playing, like the Society Cafe.

However, the picture I have tried to draw of Chicago in the 1920s is based on fact. Jazz clubs like the Society were common in Chicago of the day. Gangsters did indeed have considerable control of the city, and were beating and murdering, not only each other, but innocent people. The Black Belt, as it was called, in Chicago's South Side, was as I have described it. Furthermore, the jazz clubs and dance halls there were real. In particular, Lincoln Gardens, where King Oliver and his Creole Jazz Band played, with Louis Armstrong on second cornet, was real and was as I have given it in the book. Besides Oliver—who was a heavy eater—other musicians mentioned, such as Benny Goodman, Frank Tesche-macher, Jimmy McPartland, Sidney Bechet, Bud Freeman, Lawrence Duhé, and Bix Beiderbecke, were all playing around Chicago at the time in the places discussed. Most of them went on to become important figures in jazz history, although at the time of the story they were just beginning to be known. In particular, the New Orleans Rhythm Kings, which recorded first in 1922, had developed a following of jazz fans and young musicians like McPartland and Freeman. Just like Paulie, they were learning how to play jazz by copying the Rhythm Kings' records.

Perhaps more important than the factual details are the intangibles, the attitudes and feelings of the people of the day towards jazz and the world in general. The United States was, as it is today, home to millions of recent immigrants and their children, who were struggling one way or another to come to terms with the new world in which they found them-selves. Most of the newcomers worked at the hardest kind of jobs, and many of them lived in poor neigh-borhoods. They reacted to their circumstances in various ways. A good many returned to the countries they had come from. Others simply struggled to get by from day to day. Yet others were determined to succeed in their new homeland, and like Frank Hor-vath, worked long hours at trades and businesses to advance themselves. Like Frank, these people wanted to see their children climb a step up the ladder, and were not always happy when their children chose paths that did not seem to lead to social and financial success.

Attitudes towards jazz, then, were mixed. Many young people saw this exciting new music as representative of what they felt was a new spirit coming into American life—a spirit of freer emotions and personal expression. Others saw the music as part of the breakdown in morals they felt was occurring at the time. What particularly bothered these people were the new dances being done to jazz, which seemed to them too sexy. But many felt that jazz music itself had the ability to corrupt the morals of the young.

Regretfully, the United States was then still racially segregated in a way young people today may not understand. Blacks could not eat in restaurants meant for whites, work at many jobs alongside whites, play in big league sports teams (blacks had their own leagues), sit in theaters beside whites. Many whites, like Paulie's parents, felt that blacks were beneath them, and thus disliked jazz because it was, as they saw it, "nigger music."

What of Paulie's future? Through the 1920s jazz continued to rise in popularity, until by the end of the 1920s top jazz musicians were making very good salaries—in some cases far more than Paulie's father could make in the plumbing business. In 1929 the stock market collapsed, and the Depression that followed hurt jazz along with everything else. But in 1935 there came a boom for swing bands, some of which played a lot of excellent jazz. Again it was possible for jazz musicians to make good livings. In fact, some leaders of popular swing bands, like Benny Goodman and Duke Ellington, became quite wealthy.

Thus, if Paulie continued to work hard at his music, there is every chance that he could have made a successful career in jazz, although it is undoubtedly true that at times he might have had to play more commercial kinds of music to keep going. Would his parents have been happy about this? It would be interesting to guess.

Readers who want to hear some of this early jazz should be able to find it with a little searching. The records of the Original Dixieland Jazz Band, the King Oliver Creole Jazz Band, Bix Beiderbecke and the Wolverines, and the New Orleans Rhythm Kings have been reissued in various formats. Many libraries have jazz record collections, and they may include some of the above. However, I must warn readers that this very early jazz will be disappointing at first hearing. The music will be unfamiliar; and worse, the records were cut before the advent of electrical recording and lack the clarity we take for granted today.

My suggestion, therefore, is to start with somewhat later recordings of these jazz greats, which are more easily available in libraries and on CD and tape. They are also better recorded. I would particularly recommend Louis Armstrong and his Hot Five and other groups from 1925 to 1928; King Oliver and his Dixie Syncopators from 1926 on; and various Bix Beiderbecke groups under his own name made in 1927 and 1928. It might also be interesting to hear Frank Teschemacher, whom Paulie sat in with, although you will probably need some help from somebody familiar with this older music in ferreting out the records he appears on. This later music is a little different from the music of the earlier bands that Paulie was hearing, but it is close enough. In any case, it is the sort of music he would have been playing by the time he became a professional a few years later. That is, of course, if he did not decide to go into the plumbing business after all.

—*James Lincoln Collier*